This is a really creative way of communicating the Christian faith to Muslims. During their many years of work in Yemen and other places in the Middle East, Bernie and Catherine Power have clearly mastered the art of telling stories, not only to respond to the many objections and challenges presented by Muslims, but to present the basic truths of the gospel in positive and imaginative ways. This approach is undergirded with serious study of the Qur'an and Hadith, and by sensitivity to the cultures of Islamic communities. If Jesus told stories (parables), why shouldn't Christians today do the same?

Colin Chapman
Author of *Cross and Crescent: Responding to the Challenges of Islam*

In his latest book, Bernie Power draws on his own rich experiences in the Arab world over more than two decades to provide a wealth of resources for Christian apologists in Muslim contexts. The book is grounded in scholarly source material, with copious references to both the Bible and Qur'an. The centrality of a storytelling approach makes this book eminently readable and ensures its relevance to Christian–Muslim interaction in diverse contexts.

Dr Peter Riddell
Australian College of Theology

God's love, God's grace and God's forgiveness beautifully told in a simple story about telling simple stories. An entertaining and insightful way of uncovering profound truths hidden by cultural conditioning. This book will release a wonderful gift to the Muslim world, as Bernie masterfully applies his wisdom for evangelism and apologetics revealing the Jesus sent for all humanity.

Neil Johnson
20Twenty (Vision Christian Radio)

In this book Bernie Power offers practical examples of stories and other approaches that can be used to present the good news to Muslims. These are set in an overarching narrative account, which includes both the narrator's journey into using stories in evangelism and examples of different responses. Helpfully included are also some instances of storying in women's contexts. This book will be immediately useful: it forms a great addition to his earlier works.

Dr Moyra Dale
Author and speaker on Islamic issues

About the author

Bernie Power has been studying Islam and interacting with Muslims for over 40 years. He has degrees in Science, Arts and Theology, and his doctorate compared the Hadith, the early traditions about Muhammad, with biblical teaching. He currently lectures at the Melbourne School of Theology in Islamic studies. Bernie, his wife Catherine, a medical doctor, and their two sons worked as Interserve partners in Pakistan, Jordan, Oman and Yemen for over 20 years. Today Bernie engages with Muslims in Australia, and this includes public debates with Islamic scholars. He travels to many countries to teach about Islam and to share the good news with Muslims. He has written three books on the Muslim–Christian interface. Bernie's passion is to teach Christians about Islam, and Muslims about Jesus.

Storytellers

Bringing Muslims Home

BERNIE POWER

Published by Acorn Press, an imprint of Bible Society Australia.
ACN 127 775 973
GPO Box 4161
Sydney NSW 2001
Australia
www.acornpress.net.au

ISBN 9780647531013 (pbk); 9780647531020 (ebk)

Scripture quotations are taken from the Holy Bible, New International Version® Anglicized, NIV® Copyright © 1979, 1984, 2011 by Biblica, Inc.® Used by permission. All rights reserved worldwide.

 A catalogue record for this book is available from the National Library of Australia

NATIONAL LIBRARY OF AUSTRALIA

Edited by Cassie Holland
Cover and text design by John Healy
Drawings by Ivan Smith

CONTENTS

Introduction

The Middle Eastern moon shone brightly. On the spacious flat roof of a house in the centre of the city, about fifty men sat around a large fire that was burning in a brazier. It was winter – a bit chilly, but still pleasant enough. Soon, the men would eat, plunging their hands into large communal plates of aromatic rice piled high with goat meat and garnished with vegetables. Spiced sweets, dates and fruit, and sweet tea were waiting on the side. In one corner of the roof, a man was tuning up a melodious eleven-stringed oud, flanked by two men gently tapping on goatskin tablas. The singing and dancing would start soon.

Seated among them was a man with a brown beard. Like all the other men, he wore a long, white thobe and the local headscarf. He stood up and spoke, in foreign-accented Arabic, 'Ahlan wa sahlan ila bayti.' (Welcome to my home.)

They replied in chorus, 'Ahlan bik, ya Doctor Tammam.' (Welcome to you, Doctor Tom.)

The foreigner continued, 'In past days, the Arabs had no TV or radio. They used to gather on nights like these around a fire to tell each other stories.'

'It was better then,' one called out.

'Yes,' said Tom. 'So tonight, we will revive that old tradition.' The men cheered and clapped. Tom smiled and silently thanked God for this opportunity. Tonight, he would tell a story that could change their lives.

In the room below, Hannah was seated in the midst of a group of twenty veiled women. She also wore a veil. Hannah knew many of the women as patients in the small medical practice she ran from her house. Like her husband, Tom, she had been preparing for this occasion for several years. She, too, was a storyteller. She began the evening with the story of Jesus healing the woman who suffered from continual bleeding. The women listened attentively, absorbing every detail. This story spoke deeply to so many of them.

1

Telling the good news to Muslims through story

Muslims, like most people, love stories. They are easily drawn into the drama, identify with the personalities, savour the tensions that arise, and hope for a good outcome. The humour, heroism and resolution attract them, whereas abstract theology may leave them cold. A discussion built on theoretical concepts without practical illustrations is like serving up simple boiled meat and vegetables with no seasoning or spices: it is probably healthy enough, but lacks the flavour to make an appetising, enjoyable and memorable meal. Ideas separated from context are like the skeletons in a museum or dissected body parts in a laboratory. They may be helpful for biological classification, but they are lifeless. Such dead things have little appeal for Muslims – they would much rather interact with the living. A story brings characters and events and even ideas to life. A storyteller will draw a crowd; a well-told tale can hold an audience.

This book outlines ways of presenting the good news of Jesus Christ to Muslims and answering their many questions in story form. The aim is to see Muslims come home to the true biblical Jesus they learn about only partially and imperfectly in the Qur'an.

The common cultural links between the Middle Eastern Jews of Jesus' day and the Arab Middle East origins of the now worldwide religion of Islam suggest that this approach is warranted. And it is not untried theory. The narrative theology approach arises from this author and his wife's four decades of experience in working with Muslims, including over twenty years living and working in Muslim-majority countries in Asia and the Middle East.

1. How It Started

Tom Harrison sat stiffly in his chair, looking at the large oak door. He was feeling nervous. The door opened and Professor Taylor beckoned him in, greeting him warmly. Tom had been in this office many times. The book-lined shelves, the view of the campus out of the large bay window, and a pile of papers on Professor Taylor's desk were familiar. But there was some tension in Tom's mind. This was his final subject of his bachelor's degree and he was anxious about the result. Professor Taylor picked up the theology paper, thumbed through it, and smiled.

'This is excellent, Tom. As usual,' he began. 'You have shown a very clear understanding of the Westminster Confession. Another High Distinction – congratulations. You are a very clear thinker and a good writer. You could have a great future in academia if you wanted.'

Tom relaxed – his shoulders loosened. He was pleased and embarrassed at the same time. He smiled. 'Thank you. I enjoyed preparing it,' he replied quietly. 'I love the challenge of systemic theology.'

'Well, this is your last subject. So, what's next? An Honours year and, ultimately, a doctorate in theology? Your scholarship is exceptional.'

'Actually, Professor,' said Tom, 'after a lot of prayer and thinking, I am convinced that the Lord is leading me to work overseas.'

'That's wonderful,' Professor Taylor replied. 'Any part of the world in mind?'

'There's a job in Yemen that I'm interested in. I could use my PhD in chemistry and teach at a university.'

'Wow. Yemen. That will be a challenge. I imagine the first question your family and friends will ask is, "Is that safe?"'

Tom smiled. 'If you're saved, everywhere is safe.'

Now it was the professor's turn to smile. 'Nice comeback. But what do you know about Yemen?'

'It's pretty poor – below Bangladesh on most of the socio-economic indicators,' said Tom. 'The poorest of the Arab nations. An island of poverty floating in a sea of Middle Eastern oil-soaked affluence. It's a very agricultural society. About seventy to eighty per cent of Yemenis work on the land.'

'So, how might you go about sharing the gospel in that context?' asked the professor.

'Probably the same way I do with university students here. I would have to be more careful, of course. But people are basically the same everywhere. Even if people are not educated, that does not mean they are unintelligent. I would give them the information, ask them to think about it, pray for the Holy Spirit to do his work, be persistent. William Carey said, "Attempt great things for God. Expect great things from God." It'll be a tough gig. Of course, I would have to learn Arabic first.'

Professor Taylor smiled. 'Yes, that's true. But you might be missing something else, something very important.'

'What do you mean?' asked Tom.

'Well, it's about methodology. You clearly want to convey God's truth to them. Have you thought about how God communicated to us? What does the Bible show us?'

'It's the word of God. It's full of timeless and eternal truths that are applicable for every person in every place at every time,' replied Tom.

'That's true. But have you considered the format? The Bible is full of stories, spoken into specific contexts. About seventy per cent of the Bible is narrative – it is basically one long story.'

Tom frowned. 'Yes, but if you want to get to the foundational doctrines, you need to isolate the basic principles. That's what the Westminster Confession is all about.' He motioned towards to his systematic theology paper on the desk between them.

'Again, true,' replied the professor, 'but that is a historical and cultural expression of the teaching of the Bible. Western thinking is often based on the dualistic Greek concept of mind being more important than matter. Maybe that won't work so well in Yemen.'

Tom was confused. 'Do you have another suggestion?' he asked.

'Let's think about Jesus' teaching. How do you classify it?'

'It was very egocentric, if I can use that term – but in a positive kind of way. Look at the "I am" sayings, the long discourses about his identity, the controversies with the Pharisees and Sadducees and others. Jesus was very clear about his divine sonship.'

'Again, very true,' said the professor, 'but not the whole story. What you cited was mostly from John's Gospel. It is interesting that the context for much of the teaching of John's Gospel was in Jerusalem among the educated elite. But in the synoptic Gospels of Matthew, Mark and Luke, Jesus used a completely different approach. What was it?'

'Oh. The parables. Of course,' Tom felt caught out. How could he have missed that?

'Yes,' said the professor. 'That was Jesus' distinctive style of teaching in rural Galilee. He used the situations that people were familiar with to teach God's deepest truths, and crowds were amazed and delighted. Both Matthew[1] and Mark[2] report that "he did not say anything to them without using a parable". Storytelling has a long and distinguished history. From what you have told me about Yemen, perhaps you could consider that.'

THE TOPIC WAS IMPORTANT
BUT TOM'S ATTENTION WAS WANDERING...

---

1 Matt 13:34.
2 Mark 4:34.

Tom nodded, but his attention was wandering. He had too many other things on his mind at the moment. Besides the job application that was pending, there was dinner tonight with Hannah, his fiancée. She had finished her medical studies the year before and was now working as a junior doctor in a large hospital. She was committed to overseas work too. Having grown up in Africa, she knew what she might be facing. Tom, however, had travelled little. There had not been the opportunities. But he felt that God would enable him, so he faced the future with confidence. And alongside Hannah, he felt encouraged. They could tackle the challenges together.

Sensing Tom's distraction, Professor Taylor stood up.

'Tom, let me say this. Whatever you decide to do, and however you choose to do it, I reckon that you are going to have a pretty interesting life.'

Before Tom left, he thanked the professor for his teaching, advice and encouragement. His head was spinning. He had much to think about.

2. Getting Ready

'Stories are the scripts of our lives. Think about it. Your own life is experienced as a string of narratives, from the day you were born until today. If I asked you about something interesting that happened yesterday, you would most likely tell me a story.'

Dr Miriam Glenn was teaching Cultural Anthropology, her favourite subject. She was particularly pleased with this group of students. They were all aiming to work overseas in various roles. They seemed keen to learn and were quickly grasping the key issues in this course. Among the most interested were Tom and Hannah, newly married and planning to work in Yemen. Miriam had visited Yemen several times and found it fascinating. The rugged landscape of its geography paralleled the rough exteriors of its people. Yemeni men and women were typically small in stature, a product of the hard lives they lived, eking a basic subsistence out of its rocky soils. This made them very pragmatic people, not given to philosophical speculation. If something worked, it was accepted. If it wasn't practical, it was quickly discarded as useless.

A hand shot up in the class. It was Tom's.

'Excuse me, Dr Glenn. Are stories universal? Does every culture tell stories in the same way?'

'Well, yes and no. Certainly the concept is universal. You will find stories in every culture, at least in every culture that I have ever come across. However, the way that the stories are told, and the reasons for telling them, differ from culture to culture. A tale that makes sense in one country might be completely misunderstood in another. What one culture considers to be clever and wise may be thought of as totally foolish in another context. So stories may not transfer across cultures. You need to do your homework before you tell a story in a different setting. What you think is funny may be insulting and offensive in another culture. So storytelling needs to be done with care.'

Now it was Hannah's turn to ask a question.

'This might sound a bit basic, but … what is a story? And what is the purpose of a story? What are the essential elements?'

'A great couple of questions,' said Miriam. 'Let's bounce them around a bit. Firstly, what is a story? Anyone?'

'A fun way to disguise facts,' offered Peter. He was a no-nonsense engineer intending to work on dam construction in Nepal. To everyone else in the class, he seemed more at home with facts than with fun.

'Does it always have to involve "facts"?' asked Karina. She was a purple-haired ethnomusicologist whose focus of study was African drumming. 'Isn't just having fun enough by itself?'

Peter and Karina had often disagreed vociferously in class, and Miriam wanted to keep this topic a bit channelled. She intervened with a comment.

'Certainly, there are a range of different types of narratives, such as legends, and myths, and folktales. They don't always have to be believable – in fact, sometimes the less believable they are, the better the story and the greater the impact. But what common elements might we find in every story?'

'Of course, there must some characters or actors. Probably a context. Perhaps a problem or issue that needs to be resolved, and a process with a beginning, a middle and an end.' Ranji was an Indian student who had majored in Business Studies before joining this course.

'If you want to convey some important information, are there any advantages to telling a story, as opposed to just outlining the facts of the matter?' It was Peter again. This whole narrative approach seemed very inefficient to him. Stories involved too many unnecessary words. Also, they could be unclear and might be misunderstood.

'Well, there are certain advantages that I can see for "telling stories" over "stating facts",' said Karina. She emphasised the words "stories" and "facts". 'Some to them are tactical. When you are telling a story, you have the initiative. It's a bit like playing a song. Everyone wants to hear how it ends. They get involved in the process. So you are less likely to be interrupted. Secondly, a story cannot be argued with. It is not like a theological or philosophical proposition that is up for debate and disagreement. A story stands by itself. It just is.'

'Hmm … tactical. That's good. I like that,' replied Peter, rather surprised that he and Karina might agree on something.

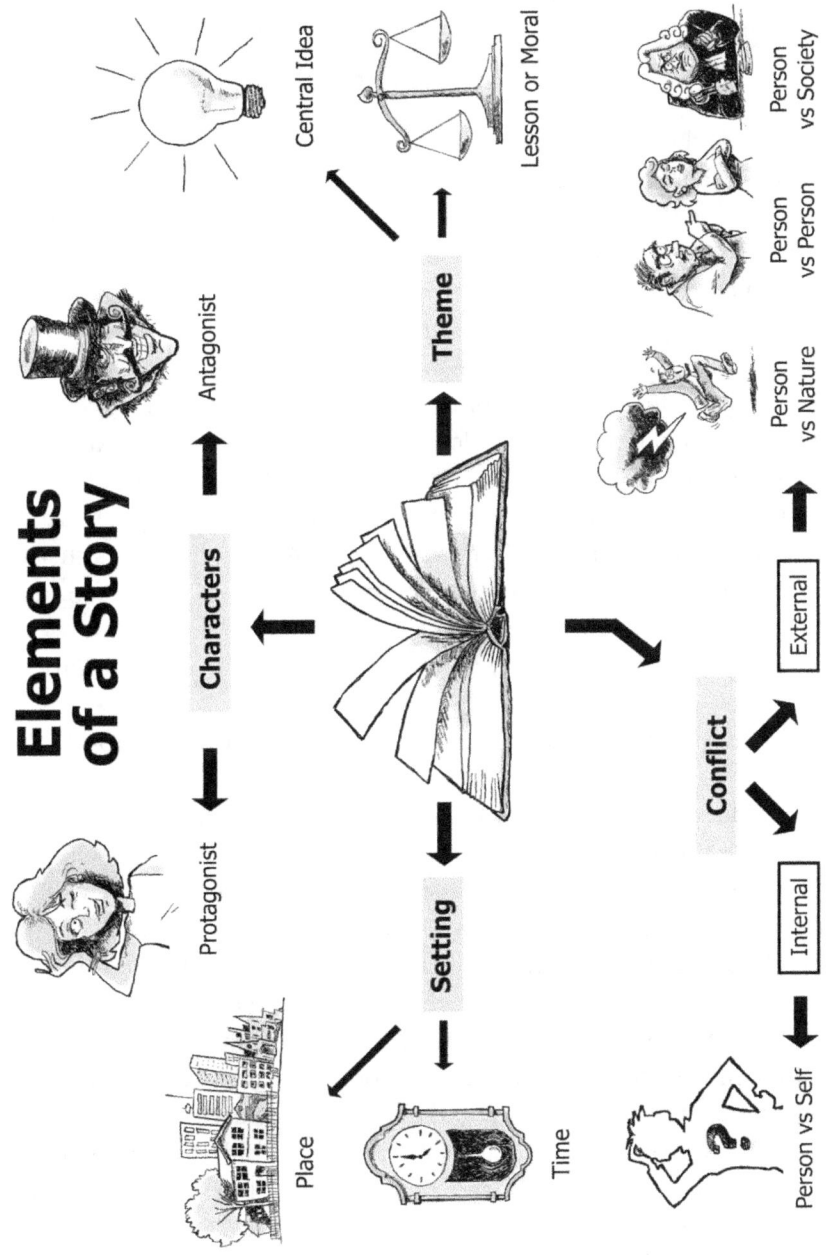

'And another thing that just occurred to me,' suggested Hannah, 'is that stories are more easily remembered, because of their structure and characters. So they are more likely to be passed on to others.'

'Ultimately, the storyteller maintains control of the story, including the meaning of the story, if there is one,' suggested Ranji.

'Yes, if there is one. But most stories do have a point, even if it is just to entertain people, as in a joke,' said Miriam. 'However, we want to be telling stories which have impact and meaning, just like Jesus' parables. So that brings me to the assignment for this course.'

There was an audible groan from the class.

'No, don't groan,' continued Miriam. 'This is going to be "fun", as Peter suggested. I want you to do some research on the country or community that you are going to and explore storytelling in that context. Find out how stories are told, who tells them, what stories are used for, that sort of thing. But make it practical. Ask yourself, "What issues might I encounter, what questions might be raised, and what is a story or stories that could communicate effectively in the face of those issues?" Make up some stories of your own that could speak into that situation.'

After the class, Hannah and Tom went up to Miriam to ask for some advice.

'Could you suggest some resources we might use for storytelling in Yemen?'

'Of course,' said Miriam. 'Yemenis love stories and Arab and Muslim culture are full of them. You could start with *One Thousand and One Nights*, or *Kalila and Demna*, both old classics. Then, there are the many witty short stories about Juha, or Goha, the wise fool. He is known as Mullah Nasreddin in Persian writings. Iner Bushnaq's *Arab Folktales* is a good resource.'

On the way home, they stopped at the city's largest bookshop and came away with several volumes. Over the next few months, they worked on this assignment, reading captivating accounts of wealthy kings, wise queens, clever peasants, wicked villains and brave heroes. Based on these tales, Tom and Hannah developed a series of stories that could answer the questions and objections that Muslims were raising to the Christian faith. Then, they began to visit the local mosques in their city and hang out at the coffee shops, which were frequented by Arab migrants. They road-tested the stories they had developed, honing them until they could tell them with confidence.

THEY VISITED THE LOCAL MOSQUE TO TELL
THEIR STORIES TO ANYONE WHO WOULD LISTEN.

One day, Tom came home jubilantly waving a letter.

'The Yemen National University has appointed me as Lecturer in Chemistry, starting next year. And they have agreed to fund six months of Arabic language study in Sana'a before I start teaching.'

In due course, their visas arrived, and Tom and Hannah boarded a plane for the Middle East. A new adventure was about to begin.

3. Who Are You?

Sana'a, the capital of Yemen, is nestled in a range of mountains that run, like a backbone, down the country's western seaboard with the Red Sea. The city's high elevation (over two-thousand metres above sea level) makes the weather quite mild all year round. The city limits are geographically contained, a relatively flat area bounded by high mountains on all sides. The old city is a collection of tall, medieval, pink-brown mudbrick buildings, clustered closely together and gaudily decorated with white plaster, giving them the appearance of gingerbread houses. They are joined by narrow, stone-cobbled streets. Tall, stone, medieval walls surround the buildings and streets of the old city, a reminder of its violent past. Now, outside the walls, new suburbs have sprouted, consisting of more modern stone or concrete buildings.

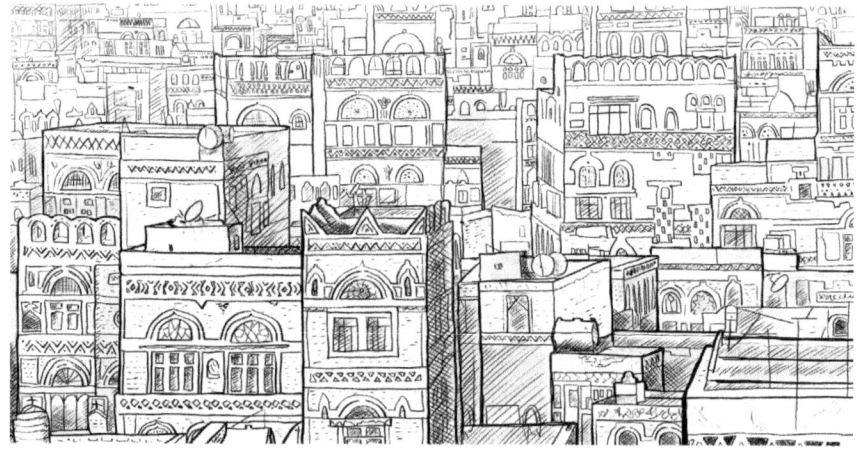

THE OLD CITY LOOKED LIKE A COLLECTION OF GINGERBREAD HOUSES.

Tom and Hannah were met at the airport by a small delegation from the university and taken to their house. It was a furnished second-floor apartment located in a bustling suburb, a short walk from the university.

Sana'a has maintained much of its traditional feel, and most people still wear local Arab clothing. Tom and Hannah wanted to identify with their new culture as much as possible. So they decided to wear the national dress, in the same way that most immigrants to Australia wear Western clothes. A couple of Tom's new university colleagues took him to a men's clothing shop and fitted him out with his long white *thobe* and a white Arab headscarf. They showed him how to put it on.

'You look just like a Yemeni,' declared one of his colleagues. 'From now on, we should call you "Doctor *Tammam*". It means "excellent"!'

Hannah was taken by their wives to a women's clothing shop next door and emerged wearing an all-enveloping black *balto* and a colourful hijab. Her name was very close to the Arabic name *Hanaa*, which means 'happiness', so she accepted it. As they walked out onto the street in their new clothing, Tom and Hannah almost blended in. However, their light-coloured skin and eyes gave them away as foreigners.

THEIR LIGHT SKIN COLOUR AND EYES
GAVE THEM AWAY AS FOREIGNERS

13

The next day, they walked down to a public park near their house. As they drew near, they saw TV cameras and many people sitting on a stage, surrounded by a large crowd. It was a variety entertainment show, with inspirational speakers, comedians and singers, live streamed on national television. A man with a clipboard spotted them and asked them where they were from – foreigners were rare in this part of town. He asked if they would like to give greetings from their country to the audience. They agreed. As they were led onto the stage, one of the announcers proclaimed in English,

'This is Doctor Tammam and his wife Hanaa. They have come from Australia to give us their greetings, and they have become Muslims!' The crowd of several hundred leapt to their feet and started clapping and cheering loudly.

Tom walked up to the microphone and waited for the noise to die down. In a loud voice, he stated, 'Thank you. It is wonderful to be here with you today. We bring you greetings from our country. But there has been a mistake. We are not Muslims. We are followers of Jesus Christ. However, we are very glad to be here. May God bless you!'

The crowd went silent. The announcers looked at each other, embarrassed. The organiser in the suit quickly walked up and said to Tom and Hannah, 'Come with me.' They followed him off the stage. The announcers were very upset. So were some of the audience, who gathered around them.

'Why did you say you were Muslim?' they asked.

'We never said that. No-one even asked us about our religion,' Tom replied.

One old man was particularly vehement. 'So why are you wearing Yemeni dress if you have not converted to Islam? Yemen is a Muslim country.'

Tom turned to him. 'I thought Yemen was a free country. Can't people wear what they want?' Most of the group walked off disgustedly.

But one man stayed behind. 'Could we go and have some tea?' he asked. They walked to a nearby cafe and sat down.

Abdu had a long beard and a kind face. He looked compassionate. As their tea was being served, he asked about their background, and how they were enjoying their stay in his country. Then he got down to business.

'I was just wondering, if you have chosen to live here and you are enjoying it so much, why haven't you become Muslim?' he asked, in an inquisitive tone.

Tom countered, 'If you went to Australia and decided to live there, would you become a Christian? Or if you went to India, would you decide to become a Hindu?'

'Of course not. I wouldn't change my religion just because I changed my location,' replied Abdu.

'Neither will we. For us, religion is a matter of personal choice, not because you were born in a particular place.'

'Yes, that's true,' said Abdu. 'Our Holy Qur'an says, "There is no compulsion in religion".[1] But it also says, "Whoever seeks a religion other than Islam, it will never be accepted of him, and in the Hereafter, he will be one of the losers".[2] Do you want to be a loser?'

Tom thought that a circuit-breaker was necessary. So he asked, 'Abdu, would you like me to tell you a story?'

'Of course,' said Abdu. 'I love stories. Please tell it.'

'There was once a beautiful palace. It was exquisite in every way – marble floors, golden walls, and jewels everywhere. It was the most stunning place you could imagine. Now, there was a man who lived in that attractive palace, but he was not a happy man. Every morning he woke up in fear. You see, he was a slave and his job was to scrub the floors of the palace. As he toiled each day, he worried if his work was good enough. He wondered if the king would accept it. If the work was not good enough, and the king got angry, the slave could be punished and thrown out of the palace. And then where would he live and what would he do?

'But there was another man who lived in the palace, and every morning he woke up full of joy. He was the prince, the son of the king. The king loved his son and talked with him every day. The son knew that he belonged in the palace forever and would never be asked to leave, because his father was the king.' Tom stopped for a breath.

Abdu jumped in. 'That is an interesting story, but what does it mean?'

---

[1] Q 2.256. Quotes from the Qur'an will appear in this format: Q x.y, where x is the chapter, and y is the verse.

[2] Q 3.85.

Tom paused, then said: 'Abdu, it is a story about choices. If you had the choice, who would you rather be: the slave, or the son?'

WHO WOULD YOU RATHER BE: THE SLAVE OR THE SON?

'Certainly, I would want to be the son. No-one would want to be the slave.'

'So,' Tom went on. 'If you were the son, would it make sense to try to become a slave?'

'Of course not!'

Tom explained, 'Jesus said, "A slave has no permanent place in the family, but a son belongs to it forever".[3] However, the Qur'an says, "No-one comes to Allah except as a slave".[4] So, Abdu, in asking me to become a Muslim, you are asking me to exchange my position of privilege and love as his son in God's kingdom for a position of slavery under Islam. As a follower of Jesus, I am a child of God. Why should I exchange the guaranteed grace and acceptance of God? Islam is an uncertain religion of trying to do enough good works to earn Allah's favour. Personally, I think I would make a very poor slave. I would most likely fail to be good enough, so it just wouldn't make sense for me to change.'

---

3 John 8:35.
4 Q 19.93.

Tom continued. 'There is another thing. The Bible teaches that anyone who puts his hand to the plough and turns back is not fit for the kingdom of heaven. If a Muslim turns away from Islam, he might lose his life, but for a follower of Jesus, there is much more at stake: my salvation and an eternal relationship with God should not be given away. This is too important for me to risk losing.'

At that point, Abdu's face darkened. 'If that is your view, you are welcome to hold it. As for me, all I could ever hope to be is a slave in Allah's kingdom. That is what he has made me to be. Goodbye.' And he stood up and walked off.

Tom was surprised and shaken by the abruptness of this response. He turned to Hannah, 'Oops, that didn't go too well, did it?'

Hannah frowned. 'Perhaps you could have been a bit more gracious or cautious or something. You don't have to convey everything to everyone at the first meeting. If you had been a bit more patient, you might have got another chance.'

Tom defended himself. 'Well, he was playing hardball with me. Why shouldn't I push back?'

'Because it is not a football match! It's much more important than that,' said Hannah. They walked home in stony silence. Once home, Hannah lay down on the bed, still recovering from jetlag. As the sun set, she fell asleep.

That evening, Tom went for a walk by himself in the neighbourhood. He passed two men who looked intently at him. It was dark, and he moved on quickly. Then he heard some footsteps behind him.

'Excuse me, sir.' He stopped and turned. It was the two men. One of them said, 'We saw you on television today. It seemed a bit awkward.'

'Yes, it was awkward,' replied Tom.

'Never mind,' said the shorter of the two men. 'No harm done. At least you got on TV. Now that you're famous, would you like to have a drink at our place? It's nearby.'

Tom wasn't sure why, but he quickly agreed. They went down the street and into an apartment block. As they walked up the echoing concrete stairs, Tom told them, 'My place is just two doors away.'

One of them said, 'We know. We saw you moving in.'

These two men, who introduced themselves as Yousef and Umar, would turn out to be the most un-Islamic Muslims Tom would ever meet. As they entered the flat, Tom noted that the furnishings were very Western and very tasteful. It looked like a photo shoot out of *International Home* magazine.

'I'm an interior designer,' explained Yousef, noticing Tom's interested expression.

'And I'm an artist,' said Umar, pushing the door shut. 'Meet my Swedish girlfriend, Elsa.' Behind the door was a life-size poster of a blonde, topless woman in a provocative pose.

Tom didn't know how to respond.

'Don't worry,' said Umar. 'Elsa and I have a purely platonic relationship. And in Ramadan, I cover her up with a tea towel.' He laughed. 'Now how about that drink.'

Yousef opened a sideboard revealing a wide array of whiskey and wine and beers.

'What's your poison?' he asked.

'Do you have a Coke?' asked Tom. Yousef poured a Coke for Tom, and a glass of scotch for himself. Umar twisted the cap off a small bottle of beer.

Yousef and Umar were keen to know what happened after the TV incident. Tom told them about Abdu, including the son/slave story.

Their response to Abdu was dismissive. 'Long-bearded idiots. They put our women in black bags and claim they are protecting them. They have ruined our country. But *your* story was cute – very nice, very subtle,' said Yousef.

'I have a good one you can tell next time,' said Umar. 'I heard this from an Egyptian comedian. Do you want to hear it?'

'Of course,' said Tom. 'I need something to cheer me up.'

Umar smiled and licked his lips in anticipation.

'There was a Hindu who lived in a Muslim village in India. He was the only *kaafir* (unbeliever) there. So, the imam of the mosque came to the Hindu's house to invite him to accept Islam. The Hindu gave the imam three reasons why he should not become a Muslim. "Firstly, as I walk home from work, I see the apples in my neighbour's tree and occasionally, I take one. That's stealing, which is forbidden in Islam. Secondly, when I get home, I sometimes need a drink, so I have a little nip of scotch. And alcohol is forbidden in Islam. And thirdly, sometimes I make a decision, but later, I change my mind, so I might not remain a Muslim for very long."

"Don't worry about those things," replied the imam. "Islam has a solution to every one of them. Simply recite the shahada (confession of faith) and all will become clear."

'Encouraged by this, the Hindu repeated after the imam, "*la ilah illa allah Muhammad rasul Allah.*" (There is no god except Allah: Muhammad is the messenger of Allah.) Then the imam grabbed the man's arm and said, "OK, now that you are a Muslim, you have to obey the rules or you will be punished. If I catch you stealing anything, I'll have your hand cut off. If I catch you drinking alcohol, I'll have you whipped. And if you try to leave Islam, I will have your head cut off."'

Umar turned to Tom. 'So, if someone asks you to become a Muslim, tell them you can't because it is too dangerous. You might lose your head.'

'And your brains!' added Yousef. At this, Umar and Yousef laughed loudly, high-fiving each other.

'Would you tell a story like that, Tom?' Umar asked.

Tom was still smarting from the exchange with Abdu in the morning, and the discussion with Hannah afterwards, so he wasn't ready to commit to this.

'I'm not sure. I would have to ask my wife,' he replied hesitantly. This made the two men laugh even more.

'Look,' said Yousef, 'every Saturday night we play cards and smoke *shisha* here. Would you like to join us?'

Tom wanted to establish some friendships in this new country.

'Why not?' he heard himself saying. 'I'd love to come.'

4. Who's In Charge Here?

Tom and Hannah walked into the old city of Sana'a. Ancient eight-metre-high wooden gates guarded the entrance into the walled city. One of the gates still bore the imprint of a cannonball fired against it during an inter-tribal conflict centuries ago. Tom and Hannah had been through these gates almost every day since they had arrived five months earlier.

THE MAIN GATE OF THE OLD CITY WAS IMPRESSIVE.

A local vendor saw them looking at the huge entrance. 'Those gates are big enough for an elephant to go through,' he told them.

'Elephants! There are no elephants in Yemen. That's in Africa,' Hannah replied. She was modestly wrapped in a headscarf, her body covered in a black *balto*. Encouraged by the rowdy exchanges she saw between local women and male vendors, Hannah was not afraid to talk to men in public.

'Yes, that's where they came from. The *habashiyiin* (Ethiopians) brought them over to attack our holy Ka'aba in Mecca in the year our Prophet Muhammad, peace be upon him, was born.'

Interesting story. I'll check that one out tonight, thought Tom, as they moved off.

The narrow laneways of the old city were crowded with people and goods. Piles of brightly coloured fruits and vegetables, freshly picked from the gardens inside the city wall, lay on the ground underneath fly-covered meat hanging from racks. The nearly severed heads were left on the carcasses – here, a goat, there, a calf, and a large camel's head at the end. The smell of roasted coffee beans in roughly woven baskets competed in the 'aroma-sphere' with spices and very expensive frankincense from the south of the country. Men called out the prices of their goods in a singsong voice, while women shoppers bargained loudly with them at their stalls. Children shouted at each other and at no-one in particular as they played football in a rubbish-strewn, dusty vacant lot. It was sandwiched between two ornate pink-and-white-coloured buildings. The sights, smells and sounds had initially been an overwhelming assault on the senses for Tom and Hannah, but they were now becoming familiar.

The language school was located in a side street, which muffled the constant outside noise. The concrete courtyard was filled with flowering pot plants, making a pleasant green oasis. As they entered, Yahya, the guard, greeted them while puffing on a cigarette. He always looked as if he had spent the night drinking heavily, which may or may not have been true. Alcohol of all kinds was readily available if you knew where to look, and most Yemenis seemed to know.

Their classroom was on the second floor, up a tightly turned twirl of well-worn concrete steps. The room was small, only two by three metres, hardly big enough for the small table and five chairs that crowded into it. The other students were already there. Eamon, a redheaded Irishman, worked with a United Nations-sponsored NGO (Non-Government Organisation) in community development. Carol was an American who had converted to Islam. She had met a Yemeni student at her college in the US and married him. From her discussions with Hannah outside class, it was clear that Carol was finding her new life in Yemen difficult.

Their Yemeni teacher, Adil, was predictably late. Ten minutes after the class was due to start, his motorcycle chugged into the courtyard. He ran up the stairs, and muttered, 'Sorry. I have family problems.' This was his excuse every day – family life in Yemen was, apparently, both complicated and problematic.

The lesson began with a review of the previous day's homework, and some new vocabulary about shopping. Then it was time for Qur'an reading.

This involved Adil reciting the verses in a melodious voice and the students trying to copy him. Adil seemed more interested in them getting the sound right than understanding the meaning of the words. He corrected them rigorously; not a vowel could be mispronounced.

'This is the holy word of Allah,' he told them. 'You have to say it properly.'

Tom was a bit impatient with this part of the lesson. The Arabic used in the Qur'an was not the same as that spoken in the streets or even in the books and newspapers they were starting to read. The words were as archaic as Chaucer's English and the amount of time spent on this class could be better spent on other things. So he decided to make a suggestion.

'Adil, it is great that we are learning about your holy book. But, I wondered, seeing that we students are all from Western backgrounds, whether we could do some stories from the Bible?'

Eamon snorted. 'The Bible? I've never read it before, and I am not about to start now. C'mon, Tom, we're in Yemen now, not some Bible Belt in the West. When in Rome, you know … also, we need to respect their culture and history.'

'It's not about culture or history or respect,' replied Tom. 'We're here to learn Arabic, and I'm thinking that a Bible passage that we are all familiar with might be more helpful for us linguistically at this stage.'

'Actually, I would have a big problem with that,' said Carol. She did not often speak up in class. 'There is a significant difference between the Bible and the Qur'an. The Qur'an is the holy word of Allah that has been perfectly preserved through the centuries. The Bible is the word of men, and it changes all the time. Every year, a new edition comes out. It can't be trusted because it has been altered. I would be very uncomfortable learning anything from a corrupted book.'

'I'm sorry,' said Tom, 'but I find that a bit offensive. How can you claim that the Bible is corrupted? Where is your evidence?'

Eamon jumped in. 'I may not have read the Bible, but I am aware that many German scholars, some British ones too, have challenged the Bible. My Yemeni friends tell me that the Qur'an has not been changed, but there are serious questions about the Bible. I don't think we should waste time studying it.'

Adil smiled triumphantly, surprised that he did not need to take a stand on this. 'Well, that's it then. You have my vote too, so it's a majority. Isn't democracy a beautiful thing?' he said with a slight hint of sarcasm.

Hannah frowned. No-one had even asked her what she thought. But Tom was totally deflated. He didn't quite know how to deal with this, so he went quiet.

The next part of the lesson was storytelling, where the students related a story in Arabic about something they had seen or heard. It was Tom's turn today. He began.

'This is a political story about Yemen's President, Ali Abdullah Saleh.'

Everyone knew about the President's forty-year reign where he had kept his critics at bay via bribes, intimidation and the occasional assassination. He had complete grip on power in the country. Adil got up, walked across the room and, with an exaggerated dramatic flourish, shut the door. He then sat down, smiled broadly, and whispered, 'OK. Now we are ready to hear your story.'

Tom continued, 'One day, the President wrote a book called, *My Son, Ahmed*. It told its readers about the virtues of the President's oldest son who, we all know, is being groomed to succeed him. The book described Ahmed as a hard-working, intelligent and honest man. The President had copies of this book printed and sent all around the country – every school, every office and every government department was given a free copy.'

As he told the story in Arabic, he stumbled over some words, and Adil helped and corrected him.

Tom went on. 'However, the opposition, the Islah party, was not happy with this. So, they had a book printed with the same cover, same title and same appearance, and even the President listed as the author, but the content inside was different. In their version, Ahmed was described as a lazy, womanising alcoholic. The opposition then sent their agents out to collect every copy of the President's original book, destroy them, and to replace them with their corrupted copies so that everyone thought that this was the original book. So that's my story. But I have three questions. Firstly, would it be possible to do this? Secondly, would the President know that this had happened? Thirdly, would he and could he do anything about it?'

Eamon jumped in first. 'In regards to the first question, yes, everything is possible in Yemen. Nothing is unbelievable. As for questions two and three, as someone who works in the NGO sector and closely with government departments, I can assure you that the President knows exactly what is going on, and he wouldn't allow such an unlikely thing to happen in the first place. But if it did, heads would roll, probably literally.'

Carol looked at Tom intently. 'What are you getting at with this story? I think you have an agenda.'

Now it was Tom's turn to smile. 'Of course I have an agenda. Everyone has an agenda. Yesterday the claim was made that the Bible has been corrupted. There was an original correct version, but apparently someone was able to collect all the world's copies, destroy them and replace them with another version that told a different story. So, I would ask the same three questions. Firstly, would it be possible for anyone to change every ancient copy of the thousands of Bible manuscripts, and why would they want to do that? Both Muslims and Christians accept God as the author of the earlier revelations. Secondly, would God know that such a switch had happened, and thirdly, could he or would he do something about it? If you answer "no" to these questions, then you must conclude that the Yemeni President is more knowledgeable and more powerful than God.'

Eamon saw the logic of the story. 'Brilliant,' he said.

Carol was silent. Then she said, 'Exactly. All of the previous revelations were corrupted, not by accident or human design, but by the permission of Allah. That is why it is necessary for us to have the Qur'an, the final testament. It is a book that cannot be corrupted.'

Hannah rolled her eyes. *Didn't this woman hear what was just said?* she thought.

Tom had a response. And he had done some homework. 'Could I tell another story?' he asked Adil.

'Sure, if it is in Arabic, and everyone else agrees.' They all nodded.

'President Donald Trump was very unpopular,' said Tom.

'A bit of an understatement,' said Eamon. 'He's an idiot.' Carol smiled in agreement. She had no time for her President.

Tom went on, 'So he decided to hire the best bodyguard he could, in case of an assassination attempt. He advertised throughout the world, and a very old man turned up for a personal interview. He told Trump, "I am the best person for the job – I have international experience guarding presidents during assassination attempts."

"Like who?" asked Trump.

"Protecting John F. Kennedy was my first assignment," said the man.

"You did a great job there," said Trump sarcastically. "What an epic failure!"

"Yes", the old man replied, "but that was my first job. I was young and inexperienced. I have learnt a lot since then. I left the States, and I got a job in Egypt guarding the President there."

"Which one?" asked Trump.

"Anwar Sadat in 1981."

'Trump looked puzzled – his grasp of Middle Eastern politics was not strong. An aide whispered something over his shoulder. Trump straightened up. "But he got assassinated too, didn't he?" he asked.

"Yes, that was unfortunate, but they took us by surprise. We were ready for a lone sniper, but there were four of them with hand grenades. But I learnt a lot from that experience, and I'm sure it will never happen again."

"Did they say, 'You're fired!'?" asked Trump, smirking.

"Yes, they did, but I got another job, this time in Pakistan."

"God help you. That's scraping the barrel," said Trump. "How did that work out?"

"It was going well until the presidential election of 2007," said the old man, rather mournfully.

'Trump had no idea who might have been in power then. "Give me a name," he demanded.

"I was protecting Benazir Bhutto," said the old man. The aide again leaned over and whispered into Trump's ear again. Trump's face went red. "She got assassinated too?" he said slowly and incredulously.

"Yes, a suicide bomber," replied the old man. "How could we anticipate that? But I learnt a lot from that exp…"

"Learned a lot!" roared Trump. "You have to be joking. You learned nothing! You have failed spectacularly three times. And now you come in here, expecting I'm going to put my life into your hands, and allow you to fail a fourth time. You're fired before you're even hired. Get out of here!"

DONALD TRUMP WAS LOOKING FOR A NEW BODYGUARD.

'And so, the old man got up and shuffled off slowly with his shoulders stooped and head bowed low.' Tom paused and turned to the class and said, 'So, my question is, did Trump make the right choice?'

'Hate to admit it, but yes. You can't rely on someone who has failed so dramatically three times,' said Eamon.

Carol was a bit suspicious. 'This isn't really about Trump, is it?'

Tom smiled nervously. 'The point is, that if someone consistently fails at something they are supposed to be doing, then why should we trust them? According to the Qur'an, there are four holy books still remaining on the earth – the Jewish Torah, the Psalms or Zabur of David, the Gospel or Injil from Jesus, and the Qur'an from Muhammad. Muslims claim the first three have been changed and corrupted by humans, even though Allah promises to be the protector of his words. If he failed so dismally with the first three, how can we trust him to be able to protect the fourth?'

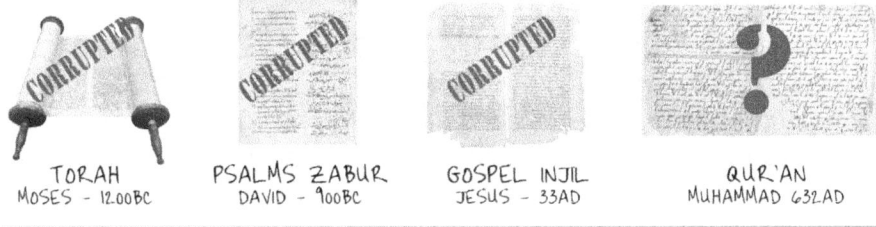

TORAH	PSALMS ZABUR	GOSPEL INJIL	QUR'AN
MOSES – 1200BC	DAVID – 900BC	JESUS – 33AD	MUHAMMAD 632AD

HE CAN'T PROTECT THREE, CAN WE TRUST HIM WITH THE FOURTH?

There was an uncomfortable silence as the significance of this sank in. Adil seized his chance.

'This has been an interesting discussion and you have all spoken very well in Arabic, so the goal of the storytelling has been successful. But I think that is enough for today. I will see you tomorrow, *inshallah.*' (Allah willing.) He stood up and walked towards the door. The class followed him out, in thoughtful silence.

Carol, however, was plotting her revenge.

5. By What Authority?

Carol had a long discussion with her husband when she arrived home that afternoon. They consulted many books. She stayed up late into the evening, doing a lot of research. She would have liked more time to prepare, but the next morning, she felt that she had enough material. Now it was her turn to tell a story in the Arabic class.

'My story is about how we got the Holy Qur'an,' she begins.

Tom and Hannah sat up expectantly. This was a surprise. Carol's knowledge of Islam was scanty at best. Eamon leaned back in his seat. He wasn't so interested, but he listened anyway. He hoped he would learn a few new words.

'In the year 610 AD, a man was sitting in a cave, fasting and meditating. His name was Muhammad, peace be upon him. Then Gabriel appeared to him, just as the angel had appeared to Mary six hundred years before. The angel recited some verses, which the Prophet, peace be upon him, repeated. These were the first verses of the Holy Qur'an, which is the literal word of Allah. It has no human intermediaries – it is the direct speech of God. Over the next twenty-three years, the angel continued to come to the Prophet to give him the wisest words that have ever been written. Muhammad, peace be upon him, then recited these words to his followers. They memorised them and wrote them down. What they wrote down is the same book that we have today. All those words, without a single change, have been perfectly preserved. So that is how we got the Holy Qur'an. Are there any questions?'

'Yes,' said Eamon. 'I have one. How is that different from the Bible?'

'It is quite different,' said Carol. 'Firstly, the Bible was not written down in Jesus' lifetime. Those who wrote it down were not eyewitnesses. We don't really know who Matthew, Mark, Luke and John were. In fact, the Bible was not finalised until the Council of Nicaea, three hundred years after Jesus left the earth. Also, the Bible has been changed many times since then. There is no copy of the original Bible, so we can never check the current versions against it to see which one, if any of them, are true.'

Tom jumped in. 'I would challenge those claims, based on historical evidence. You seem to be just repeating a lot of misinformation that you have heard from other people. None of it stands up to scrutiny.'

'Well, that's your opinion,' said Carol, 'I would expect you to say that. But the reality is that your Bible has been superseded. Even if you could prove that it was a reliable document at one time and that it had never been corrupted, it is still irrelevant. It is yesterday's news. In the Bible, you have the Old Testament and the New Testament. In the Qur'an, we have the Final Testament. It cancels out all the previous revelations. Why travel by a horse and cart, or even a car, when you can fly in a plane?' She smiled as she presented this analogy.

'That might be a good comparison if it were true, but the Qur'an itself doesn't teach that,' countered Tom. 'It says nowhere that the Bible's text has been changed. In fact, it says that the Qur'an *confirms* the previous revelations. You can look this up yourself. Here is a list of references.'[1] He handed her a piece of paper, which he dug out from his large notebook. 'You can look them up in the Qur'an yourself. It also says that God's word does not change,[2] that he protects his scriptures,[3] and that the Qur'an safeguards all the previous scriptures.[4] If you are suggesting that the Bible, which is accepted as a divine scripture by all Muslims, has been changed, then both the Qur'an and Allah have failed in their duties.'

Carol took the list, intending to show it to her husband. He would know about all these things, she thought.

Hannah could see that this discussion was not going anywhere positive. Tom, as usual, was overloading people with information, browbeating them into submission by painting them into a corner. It was time for a more subtle approach.

'Adil, could I tell a story?' she asked hopefully.

'Of course you can,' said Adil, grateful for some way to escape the increasing temperature of the discussion. 'This is the story segment, and we still have some time left.'

---

1 Q 2.41, 89, 91, 97, 101; 3.3, 50, 81; 4.47; 5.46, 48; 6.92; 35.31; 46.12, 30; 61.6; 10.37; 12.111.
2 Q 3.3, 78; 4.135; 6.34; 10.64, 115; 18.26; 35.42; 50.28, 29.
3 Q 15.9.
4 Q 5.48.

'My story,' said Hannah, 'is about an old woodcutter. He lived alone in a rough hut on the edge of his village. He was the poorest man in the village. He earned his money by going out each day to cut branches, which he brought back and sold as firewood for cooking and heating. But it was hard work as there were few trees to provide wood and he had to travel far each day.'

Everyone nodded. During their village trips outside Sana'a, they had seen such woodcutters, mostly women, carrying loads of prickly thorn tree branches on their heads.

'But one day, his luck changed. He found a clay pot under a tree. He removed the lid and out came a genie, a *jinn*. The genie was so pleased at being released from the pot that he said to the woodcutter: "I will grant any wish you desire."

'The man said, "I want to be the richest person in my village until the day I die." Suddenly four bags appeared in the genie's hands.

'The genie said to him, "Your wish has been granted. Take these bags – in them is your fortune. But do not open them until you arrive home." Then the genie disappeared.

'TAKE THESE FOUR BAGS,' SAID THE GENIE.
'IN THEM IS YOUR FORTUNE.'

'When the woodcutter arrived at his little hut, he looked at the four bags. He picked up the first bag. *It feels like it is only full of paper*, he thought. *What use is that? I can't even read.* So he put it down but he did not open it.

'Then he picked the second bag. *It feels like a brick. What use is that? I have plenty of bricks.* He put it down, but did not open it.

'He felt the third bag, but did not open it. *It feels like a bag of pebbles. What good is that? The valley is full of pebbles.*

'Then he felt the fourth bag. It felt like it was full of coins, jingling together. He opened and found it was full of silver coins. "I am the richest man in the village," he shouted. And he was.

'He bought the biggest house in the village and a white horse. Then, he got on the white horse and went around inviting the whole village to a big party at his new house. And the whole village came. He told them of his good fortune and the story of the genie granting his wish. They ate and drank and danced, and sang the praises of the old woodcutter.

'He lived well for a time, throwing a big party every night for everyone who would come, and spending the silver coins. Soon, the money began to run out. Eventually, he had to sell the white horse and the big house. And one day, the moneybag was empty, so he returned to live in his little hut on the edge of the village, but by now, he was too old to work.

'The village people said, "You cared for us when you were rich, so now, we will care for you when you are poor again." So they came to offer him food or money. Each time, he refused their help.

'He said, "No, the genie promised me that I will be the richest man in this village until the day I die."

'Eventually, he ran out of food and grew weaker. Ultimately, too proud to accept help, he died from starvation. When the people from the village came to bury him, they found in his house the three unopened bags. They picked up the first one. It was full of paper. They opened it. Inside, there were hundreds of $100 notes. The second one felt like it contained a brick. They opened it and found a large bar of gold. The third one felt like it was full of pebbles. They opened it and found dozens of large diamonds and rubies. They said, "The genie was right. He was the richest man in the village until the day he died. But because he did not open the treasures, he died as a poor man."'

'What a donkey!' said Eamon. 'But … what does the story mean? Why did you tell it?'

'As was mentioned yesterday, Muslims believe that God has given humanity four revelations: the Torah via Moses, the Zabur or Psalms via David, the Injil or Gospel via Jesus, and the Qur'an via Muhammad. This story highlights the foolishness of ignoring the richness of all that God has provided for us. The challenge is to open all the treasures that God himself has sent to us, not just one of them.'

Adil frowned. He could see the unsettling impact this story had on Carol.

'That will be all for today,' he announced.

Tom and Hannah were encouraged with the progress that they were making in the Arabic language course. Adil was a good teacher, and gave them many different ways of learning. The storytelling segment gave them great opportunities to prepare and practise the stories they had crafted back in Australia. There were still other stories they wanted to present in their class. However, they were not the only ones with an agenda.

6. An Unusual Son

Today was their last formal Arabic lesson. Tom, Hannah, Eamon and Carol had been meeting with Adil five days a week for six months. It had been very intensive, but they had all made significant progress in Arabic.

It was Carol's turn to begin the storytelling segment.

'My story is taken from the Holy Qur'an,' she said, 'and it is about Jesus. Here are the references, if you want to look them up.' She wrote the references to the passages on the chalkboard: Q 3.42–55; 5.110–118; 19.16–39; 21.91 and 66.12.

'As Muslims,' said Carol, 'we love Jesus. He is named twenty-five times in the Qur'an – nearly one hundred verses describe who he was and what he did. Jesus was born of a virgin. His mother, Mary, has a whole chapter of the Holy Qur'an named after her. She went off into a secluded place. There, she was met by the angel Gabriel who blew into her sleeve, and Jesus was conceived. It was just like when Allah blew into the dust to make Adam. The angels told her that this child's name would be Jesus, or *Isa* in Arabic, and that he would be the Messiah. She gave birth to Jesus, who spoke to her immediately, telling her to make a vow of silence not to speak to anyone that day. When she entered the village carrying baby Jesus, the villagers assumed this child was illegitimate, and accused Mary of *zina* (fornication/ adultery). But she could not speak because of her vow. So Jesus spoke up. He told them he was Allah's slave and messenger. He told people to worship Allah alone. It is also said that it is not befitting to say that Allah has begotten a son. Islam very clearly teaches that Jesus is not the Son of God. The Qur'an asks, "How could Allah have a son if he had no wife?" It seems pretty clear, doesn't it.'

The last sentence was stated with the dropped inflection of an assertion, rather than a question. Carol paused. 'Does anyone have any questions or comments?'

Hannah spoke up, 'I have a question. If Allah could not have a son because he didn't have a wife, then how could Mary have a son if she didn't have a husband? Isn't this the same logic?'

'No,' replied Carol, 'because Allah doesn't need anyone or anything else to do things for him. He simply says to something, "be" and it comes into existence. That's how Jesus was created. Just like Adam.'

This easy equivalence was too much for Hannah.

'Adam and Christ were quite different in so many ways. Adam was created from the earth, but Christ was born of a woman. Adam couldn't have parents because there were no people before him, but every other person since then has had two human parents, except Jesus. Why did God make Jesus' birth unique? Adam disobeyed God, Christ obeyed his heavenly Father. Adam's disobedience brought death; Christ's obedience brings life. The two cannot be equated as simply as you put it.'

Tom was surprised that Hannah was being so forthright. He decided to soften the tone.

'Carol, I realise that you only gave a summary, but I think you left some important parts out,' said Tom. 'You didn't mention that the angel said that Jesus would be a "pure" son, *zakiyyan*, and "among the righteous ones", *al-saalihiin*.'

'Of course, all the prophets were sinless,' replied Carol. 'That was a requirement of prophethood.'

'I'm not so sure about that,' Tom countered. 'The Qur'an catalogues the sins of Adam, Noah, Abraham, Moses, Aaron, David, Solomon, Jonah and Muhammad. I have the full list of references here.'[1] He pulled a piece of paper out of his Qur'an and showed it to her.

Carol knew better than to challenge Tom over one of his many lists taken from the Qur'an. He seemed to have a list for every occasion. 'Well, clearly, everyone has their faults and shortcomings. Only Allah is perfect,' she asserted.

'Exactly my point,' replied Tom. 'Of all the people in the Qur'an, only Jesus is described as "pure".[2] And of course, Allah is the Holy One, *al-quddus*.[3] It's one of his ninety-nine names. Another of the ninety-nine

---

[1] Adam Q 7.23, 20.121; Noah 11.47, 71.28; Abraham Q 6.76–79, 14.41, 26.82; Moses Q 28.16, Aaron Q 7.151; David Q 38.24; Solomon Q 38.35; Jonah Q 21.87, 37.142; Muhammad Q 40.55, 47.19, 48.2 c.f. Q 12.29.
[2] Q 19.19.
[3] Q 59.23.

names is *al-Khaaliq*, "the Creator",[4] and the verb "to create", *khalaq*, is used of only two beings in the Qur'an – Jesus[5] and Allah.'

'Yes,' replied Carol, 'but it also says that Jesus only created "by the permission of Allah", *bi ithn illaah*.[6] He had no power to create anything by himself.'

'Very true', stated Tom. 'Jesus himself admitted that in the Bible. He said, "I can do nothing by myself. I only do what I see my Father doing."[7] Living as a human on earth Jesus was a good and obedient son. But there were other family likenesses. For example, according to the Qur'an, Jesus also healed the sick,[8] raised the dead[9] and fed the hungry,[10] just like Allah did.[11] There were several other things that Jesus did in the Qur'an which, as the Qur'an teaches, only Allah could do.'

Eamon was enjoying this verbal sparring match and wanted to prolong it.

'What other things?' he asked.

Tom turned towards him. 'The Qur'an says that only Allah can change the law.[12] That makes sense because he is the lawgiver. But remarkably, Jesus is able to do the same.[13] Similarly, only Allah knows the hidden things, *al-ghaib*,[14] but Jesus was able to tell people what they had hidden in their houses.[15] And speaking of secret knowledge, the Qur'an says that Allah alone knows the last hour,[16] but it also admits that Jesus possesses this knowledge.[17] Moreover, Jesus isn't waiting for the last hour to know what his eternal destiny will be, as the rest of humanity must do. Jesus

---

4 E.g. Q 35.3.
5 Q 3.49, 5.110.
6 Q 5.110.
7 John 5:19, 30; 8.28.
8 Q 5.110.
9 Q 3.49.
10 Q 5.114.
11 Q 26.80, 22.6, 6.14.
12 Q 2.106.
13 Q 3.50.
14 Q 5.109.
15 Q 3.49.
16 Q 7.187.
17 Q 43.61.

is, according to the Qur'an, already in Paradise with God.[18] He alone has no sins that will need to be judged.'

'Is all that true, Carol?' asked Eamon.

She nodded weakly. Perhaps bringing up Jesus in the Qur'an was not such a good idea.

Tom wasn't finished. 'But Jesus is not just sitting unacknowledged in Paradise. The Qur'an describes him as "highly exalted in this world and the next",[19] a term used of no-one else in the Qur'an. Jesus is receiving honour and glory from those around him. And the Bible agrees on this. It says that Jesus "is exalted above the heavens".[20] It tells us what is going to happen. "Therefore God exalted him to the highest place, and gave him the name that is above every name, that at the name of Jesus every knee should bow, in heaven and on earth and under the earth, and every tongue acknowledge that Jesus Christ is Lord, to the glory of God the Father".[21] This shows that when Jesus, God's son, is honoured, then God the Father is honoured too.' Tom's voice had risen with excitement as he spoke.

'And here endeth the sermon. Thank you, Billy Graham,' said Eamon sarcastically. He felt that Tom had pushed his point too far.

But Carol had another shot. 'No doubt that Jesus could do many wonderful things because he was a prophet of Allah. We should not be surprised about this. It is not unusual.'

'I think it is,' said Tom. 'I have just listed ten things about Jesus in the Qur'an that also applied to Allah and usually only Allah. But it is significant that Muhammad did not qualify on a single one of them, according to the Qur'an.'

At the mention of his prophet, Adil felt that he had to step in. 'No! We should not compare the prophets.'

'But doesn't Allah say in the Qur'an about the prophets, "We have exalted some of them over others?"[22] And anyway, Jesus was much more than a prophet,' replied Tom. 'He was the Son of God. He said so himself.'[23]

---

18 Q 3.55, 2.255.
19 Q 3.45.
20 Heb 7:26.
21 Phil 2.:9–11
22 Q 2.253.
23 John 10:36.

'That is not a unique term to Jesus,' countered Adil. 'According to your Bible, God has tons of sons.' Adil was reading from a purple-coloured pamphlet with the Islamic Propagation Society of Yemen logo. Since this was the last lesson, he was feeling less restricted. 'Let's have a look here. Adam is called "the son of God",[24] Israel is called "God's son"[25] and his "firstborn son".[26] So is Ephraim.[27] All the people of Israel were adopted as God's sons.[28] So were the kings of Israel,[29] all Christians[30] and peacemakers.[31] So for Jesus to be called a son of God[32] was not at all unique. It looks like it was just a title shared by many others.'

Tom was prepared for this. 'Could I draw a diagram that might help explain this?' he asked.

'Of course,' said Adil. 'If you think it will help.'

Tom drew a large triangle. 'This triangle represents all living things. If we were to put all classifications of living things in this diagram, the biggest group would be what? Does anyone want to make a guess?'

Eamon jumped in quickly. 'In terms of numbers, volume and weight, worldwide, I would suggest microbes – microorganisms like bacteria, viruses, fungi and algae.'

Tom shaded in the bottom half of the triangle and labelled it "microbes".

'That's right. Perhaps half of the earth's biomass is microbic. What would the next biggest groups be?'

Eamon again, 'Probably plants, then insects.'

Tom nodded, and shaded and labelled these two categories. 'What next?'

Adil thought he should make a contribution. 'Animals.'

'Yeah, including humans,' said Eamon, a little bit sarcastically. He was hoping for a bite.

And Carol took the bait. 'Humans are not animals,' she said. 'We are a special creation of Allah, placed on earth as his representatives.'

---

24 Luke 3:38.
25 Hos 11:1.
26 Exod 4:22.
27 Jer 31:9.
28 Rom 9:4.
29 1 Chron 17:11–14.
30 John 1:12.
31 Matt 5:9.
32 John 11:27.

'But we share ninety-nine per cent of our DNA with chimpanzees. All living things are basically the same – we humans are just part of the continuum,' declared Eamon.

'All living things are not the same, and I think you know it intuitively,' Hannah spoke up. 'Imagine you ran into a burning house and could only save one thing. Would you choose an ampoule of *E. coli,* a petunia pot plant, a cup full of cockroaches, a chimp in a cage, or a baby in a bassinette?' She amazed them all with her clever alliteration. 'They are all living things, but wouldn't you save the baby and leave the others?' she asked.

Eamon looked confused. He hadn't considered this before. 'That's hypothetical, and I don't answer hypotheticals,' he said sourly.

Tom smiled at his wife's wit. 'From a Christian, and, I believe, Islamic standpoint, all creatures are NOT the same. Yes, they are all living things because they live, grow, reproduce, and die, but humans are different because they have a soul and they will live forever.'

Carol nodded supportively.

Tom added these categories to his triangle, with "Humans" in a circle at the top. 'Humans were created in the image of God. So they are living things like the others, but they are distinct. There is a difference in quality. Let's mark that by putting a circle around "humans".'

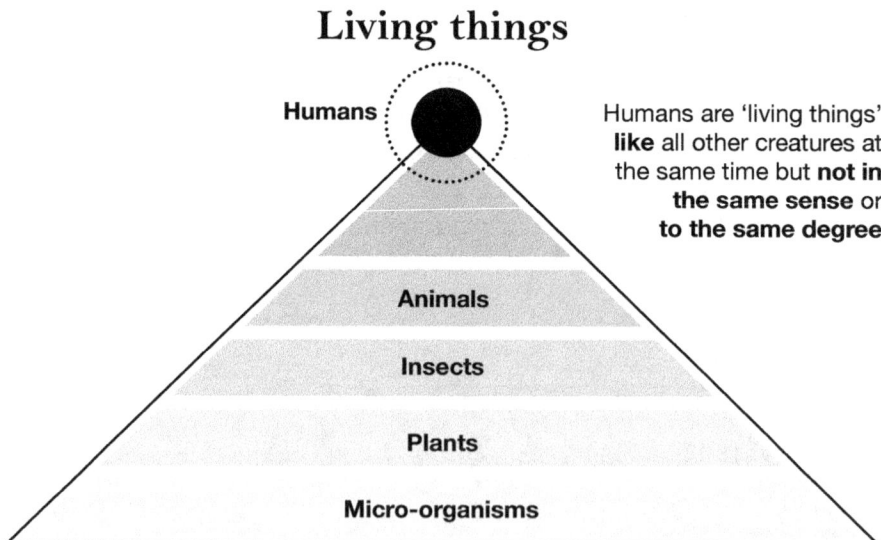

Living things

Humans

Humans are 'living things' **like** all other creatures at the same time but **not in the same sense** or **to the same degree**

Animals

Insects

Plants

Micro-organisms

'So, what has this got to do with Jesus being the Son of God?' asked Adil.

Tom drew a second triangle. He said, 'You are right in saying that God has many sons, and daughters. But, like living things, there are different categories. All people are sons of God by virtue of creation[33] and Adam is called a "son of God".[34]

He added this as a label inside the triangle. Then he went on, 'Israel is called the son of God because he was chosen by God.[35] The kings of Israel were called sons of God because they were anointed for that role.'[36]

He added these as two extra bands in the triangle. 'All Christians are called sons of God by adoption.[37] Peacemakers are called sons of God when they act like God who is a peacemaker.[38]

'But at the peak of the triangle is Jesus, who is called the Son of God because of his eternal nature. He is different from the rest, so I will put a circle around him. These are all sons of God, but not in the same sense or to the same degree.'

Sons of God

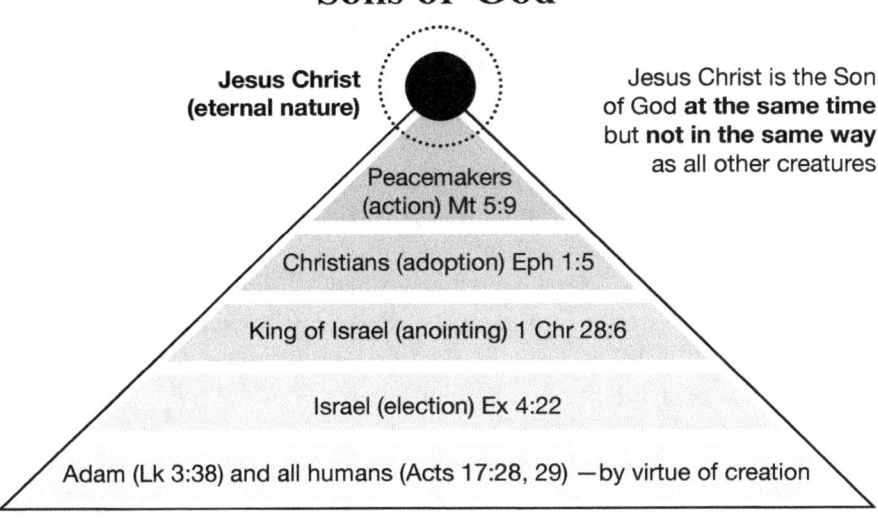

Jesus Christ (eternal nature)

Jesus Christ is the Son of God **at the same time** but **not in the same way** as all other creatures

Peacemakers (action) Mt 5:9

Christians (adoption) Eph 1:5

King of Israel (anointing) 1 Chr 28:6

Israel (election) Ex 4:22

Adam (Lk 3:38) and all humans (Acts 17:28, 29) — by virtue of creation

---

33 Acts 17:28–29.
34 Luke 3:38.
35 Exod 4:22.
36 1 Chron 17:11–14.
37 John 1:12.
38 Matt 5:9.

Adil was not convinced. 'It doesn't matter how you divide them up. Allah has no sons. The Holy Qur'an says, "He is Allah. The One. The self-sufficient. He does not beget, nor was he begotten. And there is none co-equal or comparable to Him."' [39]

'Yes, *Surat al-Ikhlas*. I know that one. And I agree that God does not sire children by sexual intercourse, nor is he the product of a sexual union. That's what the Arabic terms mean. However, the Qur'an does teach us about the reality of a non-physical son.'

'Isn't that an oxymoron?' asked Eamon. 'What other kind of son is there?'

Tom responded, 'The Qur'an describes a traveller as *ibn sabeel*, "a son of the road".[40] It is not that the road is his physical father, but rather that he takes his identity from the fact that he is on the road, and his destiny is tied up with the direction of the road. It is used in a metaphorical or symbolic way. Likewise, Jesus has his identity from the fact that he has come from God,[41] and his destiny is tied up with returning to the Father.[42] In this way, he is "the Son of God". He is the spiritual Son of his heavenly Father. Jesus said, "Flesh gives birth to flesh, but the Spirit gives birth to spirit."'[43]

Carol would not give up. 'But the Bible calls Jesus "the only-begotten Son", according to John.[44] However, the Qur'an states clearly that "It is not fitting for Allah to beget a son".'[45]

'Yes,' replied Tom. 'Some older English translations do use the term "only-begotten", but that is a misrepresentation of the Greek term *monogenēs*. It means "unique" or "one of a kind", i.e. *mono* plus *genus*. If the Greek term was *monogenetos*, which is not used in the Bible, that could be translated "only-begotten", indicating a physical or sexual origin. In Arabic translations of the Bible, Jesus is identified as *ibn allah,* "the spiritual or metaphorical or symbolic Son of God", never *walad Allah,* "the physical sexually-generated Son of God".'

'I think you are just splitting linguistic hairs,' scoffed Eamon.

---

39 Q 112.1–4.
40 Q 2.177.
41 John 13:7; 16:28.
42 John 7:33; 14:2, 21; 16:5, 28.
43 John 3:6.
44 John 1:14–18.
45 Q 19.36.

'No, these differences are important. Imagine a man goes to a public park and sees a family picnicking there. He tells them, "I pay taxes for this park, so I am an owner of this land. I want you to leave immediately." The picnickers reply, "We also pay taxes, so we are as much owners as you. Our claims to this park are equal." So the man has no authority in this situation.

NO AUTHORITY

'However, the next day, the man finds the same group picnicking on the front lawn of his house. So he tells them, "I am *the* owner of this land. Please leave immediately." He would be within his rights to demand this. He has full authority. He is in a unique status compared to them. They would have to leave because the two situations are quite different.'

FULL AUTHORITY

'So, what does this have to do with Jesus?' asked Eamon.

'Well, Jesus was not accused of blasphemy because he said, "I am a son of God, just like everyone else". This is a general claim that applies to everybody in some way. Jesus was crucified because he made an exclusive declaration. He said that he was *the* Son of God, a matchless position of honour and authority. He made many other unique assertions – he said he was the light of the world,[46] that he could forgive sins,[47] that he could give eternal life[48] and that he would judge the world.[49] But if you think about it, only God can make such absolute claims. That was why the Jews of his time tried to stone him. They said, "You, a mere man, claim to be God."'[50]

---

46 John 8:12.

47 Luke 5:22–24; 7:28.

48 John 10:28.

49 John 5:29; Matt 25:31, 32.

50 John 10:33.

Adil decided that this was enough. He announced the end of the lesson, and thanked them all for their participation in the course. They thanked him and shook hands or hugged each other. Over the six months of their course, they had grown to appreciate and respect each other, even though they didn't agree on many key issues. They promised to keep in touch.

Tom, however, was already thinking of next Monday, his first day of teaching. It would be interesting to be in front of a university class again, but in completely new circumstances.

7. We're All Poisoned!

Fifty or so students filed into the lecture room of the Yemen National University, chatting noisily. As they took their seats, the lecturer walked in, and the students fell silent. Standing at the podium was a foreigner they had never seen before. It was Tom's first day of teaching at the university.

'*Assalam alaykum wa rahmat illahi wa barakatuh*' he said. (Peace be upon you all and Allah's mercy and his blessings.)

Delighted at this Islamic greeting, the class burst into applause. They cried out, '*mashallah*' (What God has willed) and '*alhamdulillah*' (To God be the praise). If first impressions were important, Tom had nailed it.

The rest of the teaching, however, did not go as well. As he gave his carefully prepared introductory lecture on the periodic table, it was becoming clear that the English level of the students was poor. The looks on their faces and some of the questions they asked showed that they were struggling to understand what Tom was saying.

At the end of the lesson, Tom announced in Arabic, 'Tomorrow I will try to give the lecture in Arabic.' This prompted another loud round of '*mashallahs*' and '*alhamdulillahs*'. But Tom realised that he had a lot of work to do.

After the class, the dean of the university, Professor Ramzi, dropped by to meet Tom.

'Welcome to our university,' he said. He offered to show Tom around the campus. As they wandered through the different departments, Tom was introduced to the various faculty members and staff.

'Finally,' said the dean, 'I will take you to the library, such as it is.' They entered a large building. Inside, instead of open shelves full of volumes, there was a sparse collection of glass-fronted cabinets, each containing a few books, but the cabinets were locked.

'How does your borrowing system work?' asked Tom.

'Borrowing?' Professor Ramzi laughed. 'No, we never lend out our books. Students can only look at books in the library, one book at a time, and it is checked by our librarians before and after. Let me show you why.'

He took a large volume from a cabinet that had been unlocked by one of the librarians. It was called *The Illustrated Guide to Anatomy and Physiology*. As the dean flipped through the book, it was obvious that many of the glossy picture pages had been cut out and removed.

'This is what happened when we had an open borrowing system. Hence, the new restrictions. These books cost too much for us to be constantly replacing them.'

Tom didn't know quite what to say. He was embarrassed for the university, for the students, and for the country. The dean, however, did not seem to be overly concerned about this state of affairs. He appeared to accept it as normal.

That afternoon, Tom was sitting in the university cafe drinking tea when three long-bearded young men came up to his table.

'Can we join you, Dr Tom?' they asked.

'Of course,' he replied. He did not recognise them – they may have been in his morning class, but he was not sure. They sat down and introduced themselves as Ali, Bilal and Khalid. *Almost ABC*, Tom thought to himself.

'You haven't met us before. We are from the executive committee of the Islamic Students Association and we have come to welcome you to our university.' Ali was the shortest of the three and appeared to be the most confident.

'That's very nice of you. Thank you for doing that,' Tom replied.

'We have heard that you can speak some Arabic, but we are not sure if you are a Muslim or not,' Ali said.

'No, I'm not. Actually, I am a Christian,' replied Tom.

'Well, in that case, we would like to invite you to embrace Islam,' Bilal said.

Tom was a bit taken aback by this sudden and direct approach. 'Why should I do that?' asked Tom.

'Because the Qur'an is the final revelation from Allah, Muhammad is the best person who has ever lived, and Islam has produced the greatest civilisation that human history has ever seen,' Bilal continued.

'Those are pretty strong credentials,' answered Tom. 'I imagine that would make one hundred per cent Muslim countries like Yemen very wonderful places.' He was thinking back to the morning's tour of the library.

'Not necessarily,' said Khalid, frowning. 'Everybody here does not follow Islam properly. That is why we have an Islamic Students Association, even though all the students here are Muslim.'

'So having a one hundred per cent Muslim population doesn't create a perfect Muslim society?' asked Tom.

'No. None of us are perfect. We all have to do good works, and if we do, we hope that Allah will accept them and send us to Paradise when we die.' This comment came from Bilal.

'That's very interesting. Look, do you mind if I tell you a story about that?' asked Tom.

'Of course you may,' replied Ali.

Tom began. 'This story is about a man who had a serious issue that worried him very much. However, he had an old friend, a sheikh, who was very knowledgeable in religious matters as well as wise about the things of this world. He went to the sheikh's house and knocked on the door.' Tom knocked on the table six times.

'When the sheikh opened the door, the visitor blurted out his problem. "Sheikh, I am desperate! I have sinned many times and I am worried that my good works will never be enough for me to enter into Paradise. What extra good works must I do to be acceptable to God?"

'The old sheikh invited him in, and said, "Calm down. I have some insight into your problem. But first, we must sit down and drink tea."

'The visitor sat down, and the sheikh poured him a cup of tea. However, while the visitor was watching, the sheikh took out from a drawer a bottle marked "Poison" and put a single drop in the tea.'

THE OLD SHEIKH PUT A DROP OF POISON IN THE DRINK.

Tom mimicked this by taking out a pen and pretending to put a drop of ink into his own tea.

'Then the sheikh said to the man, "Please drink it."

The visitor was aghast. "I can't drink that tea. It has poison in it!"

'The sheikh smiled, and said, "Of course. I'll fix that." So, he took a teaspoon of sugar from the bowl on the table and put it into the cup of tea.'

Tom illustrated this by putting a teaspoon of sugar into his own tea.

He continued. 'Then the sheikh said, "Now drink it."

But the man said, "I still can't drink it."

'At this, the sheikh took the whole bowl of sugar and poured all of it into the cup. "There was only one drop of poison, so that should be enough sugar. Now drink it," he said.'

To the amazement of the three students, Tom poured the whole bowl of sugar into his own cup of tea to illustrate this.

He went on, 'The man said to the sheikh, "You don't understand. The issue is not how much sugar you put in the tea. The problem is the poison that is already there. How can you get rid of that?"

47

'At this, the sheikh smiled again and said, "Exactly. And that is what you are trying to do. You simply want to add more good works to your life, like the sugar. But there is a bigger problem that you have not dealt with, the poison. Our lives are like the tea. Our sins are like poison before God. Our father, Adam, committed one sin and so God expelled him from Paradise. But we have committed many sins. Even the prophet Muhammad himself said in an authentic Hadith, "No-one will enter Paradise by his good works." His companions said, "Not even you, O Messenger of Allah." Muhammad, peace be upon him, replied, "Not even me, unless Allah surrounds me with his grace and mercy.""[1]

The students knew this saying and repeated it with Tom in Arabic.

Tom continued, 'So we are not acceptable to God by our good works. Not even the prophet Muhammad could do enough good works to enter Paradise. There needs to be some way of dealing with our sins before God will accept us.'

The students went silent. They had not expected this. Finally, Khalid found some words.

'So, what is that way of dealing with sins? We've never thought of this before.'

'Well, there is one important thing to recognise. The root problem is not our outward behaviour. Our "sins" are only the symptoms. The real issue is "sin", which means putting anything else in the place of God in our lives. It is our inner rebellion against God that is the real issue. Just like the man with the poisoned drink, it is not a matter of simply fiddling with the contents. The whole glass must be tipped out, washed clean and be refilled. Jesus called it "a new birth" or being "born anew",[2] Tom explained.

'How can that happen?' asked Ali.

'It will take a while to explain it,' replied Tom, 'and I have some preparation to do before tomorrow's class. Could it wait until Monday?'

'Of course,' said Khalid. He looked at the others, and they nodded. 'And we will bring along a few others to listen to your explanation.'

'OK. Monday it is. Here. At 9 am.'

The three walked off, talking animatedly among themselves.

---

1 *Sahih Muslim* 2816f, https://sunnah.com/muslim:2816f.
2 John 3:3, 7.

8. A Crucial Meeting

Tom was second-guessing himself, once again. The invitation from the students to speak at their meeting seemed genuine. But was it a trap? Was this a wise thing to do so soon after starting this job? He wondered about discussing his reservations with Hannah, but she had just been offered a job doing village health work and had days full of meetings with Ministry of Health officials. That was absorbing all her time and attention, so Tom didn't want to worry her with his concerns. *I'm sure it will be alright*, he consoled himself.

Monday morning was bright and sunny; most days are in Sana'a are. As he walked to the university, Tom's attention was taken by the busy and chaotic scenes around him. Cars, minibuses, motorbikes, the occasional bicycle and wooden carts pulled by donkeys competed noisily for space on the congested roads. The honking of horns was incessant. However, all the vehicles slowed down and gave way to a massive trailer, overloaded with watermelons, and pulled by two haughty but moth-eaten camels. Goats picked through the rubbish that was dumped in piles along the street, and they were joined by beggars and small children who also sifted through the heaps looking for food or anything valuable. Such scenes of poverty and need no longer shocked Tom – they had become like visual white noise. He worried about this newly acquired compassion fatigue.

At the main university gate, Tom was met by Ali, Bilal and Khalid from the Islamic Students Association. 'We have organised a meeting of the Association,' said Ali. 'Everyone is looking forward to meeting you.'

Tom could hear the low rumble of many voices and it became louder as they approached the meeting place. He followed the three students inside and his jaw dropped. There were over two hundred students jam-packed into a sloping lecture theatre designed for only half that number. Every row of seats was crammed with as many people as physically possible. The overflow filled up the stairs on both sides of the lecture theatre. Others were standing on the sides at the front of the room. The last three rows at the back were filled by female students. All of them wore long black burqas – some had their heads veiled with hijabs but the majority wore niqabs, black face-coverings with a narrow slit that only permitted a pair of dark brown eyes to look out.

As soon as Tom and the 'ABC' boys entered, the students went silent. After the compulsory fiddling with microphones, the session was ready to start. Ali introduced 'Professor Tom' and declared that he was going to 'explain Christianity' to them. Tom stood up to speak, and the students leaned forward, listening carefully.

'It is good to be here in Yemen. For many years, I have dreamed of coming to your country. I have enjoyed a wonderful welcome here. This is not surprising because the prophet Muhammad (peace be upon him) said, "The people of Yemen came to you with the softest hearts and the kindest feelings. Faith is Yemeni and wisdom is Yemeni."'[1]

The students burst into applause. They knew well this famous Hadith about the Yemeni people. They prided themselves on being the first nation to accept Islam and on their reputation for generosity. They were now especially keen to hear what this foreigner had to say.

Tom continued, 'Last week, I met Ali, Bilal and Khalid and I told them a story. Let me repeat it to you.' He then retold the story of the man seeking forgiveness and his wise friend offering a poisoned drink.

'Every one of us suffers from this same problem. How can we live in ways that please God? How can we deal with our sins? Are we destined to die unforgiven? Are the fires of hell the only future that we can expect? The Bible, God's holy book, tells us that we cannot pay for our own sins. The price is too high. We need someone who is perfect to do that for us. Jesus Christ, *Isa al-Masih*, paid that price when he died on the cross for the sin of humanity.'

This assertion was too much for some of the students. A murmuring arose among them like a verbal swell. Suddenly, one of the students rose to his feet. He was holding a Qur'an aloft. He shouted out, 'No, no. Jesus did not die. The Holy Qur'an says that he did not die!'

Tom had been expecting this response, but not so soon, nor so vehemently. 'Actually, the Qur'an does not say that he did not die. It says,

---

1 *Hadith Tirmidhi*, https://sunnah.com/tirmidhi/49.

"they did not kill him, nor did they crucify him."[2] Who are "they" in this verse? If you read the verses beforehand, it is clear that these are the Jews. And it is true that the Jews did not kill the Messiah – the Roman occupiers did. The Jews had no authority to execute a criminal, so they had to go to the Romans,[3] who carried out this task for them. The normal Jewish method of execution was stoning – crucifixion was a Roman punishment. In saying that, the Jews did not kill or crucify Jesus. The Qur'an is simply affirming a fact that we know from history.'

'So, you follow a god who is dead, do you?' scoffed the interjector. The audience collectively smothered a giggle at this ridiculous concept.

Tom was prepared for this objection. 'Well, Jesus is God and he did die, but he did not mean that he ceased to exist. When you and I die, we will not cease to exist. Our death, like his death, is a mortal body going through a transition into immortality. His spirit did not die, because it lives forever. The Holy Bible says that "He was put to death in the body but made alive in the Spirit."'[4]

Tom countered with another example. 'As a Muslim, no doubt you believe that the original Qur'an, *umm elkitaab*, "the mother of the book", is in heaven. Is that so?'

'Yes,' replied the man. 'And it has been there forever.'

'So if someone took all the Qur'ans on earth and destroyed them, would this destroy the *umm elkitaab*?' asked Tom.

'No, because it is safe in heaven. The copies on the earth are only made of paper and ink,' said the young man.

'But they are still the word of Allah, according to Muslims. Likewise, when Christ died, this was not the death of God, because God lives forever. Jesus' body was killed, but his divine nature was not affected by this death. We call it not "the death of God" but "a death in God". It was like someone trying to destroy the copies of God's holy book on earth,' said Tom.

'But Jesus did not die,' persisted the student.

'Actually, the Qur'an does testify to the death of Jesus,' replied Tom. 'In the Qur'an, Jesus says, "Peace be upon me the day I am born, the day I

2 Q 4.157.
3 John 19:6–10.
4 1 Pet 3:18.

die, and the day I am raised up alive."[5] Note the order: birth, death and resurrection. Jesus spoke clearly about this. By the way, what's your name?'

'My name is Zaid,' replied the interjector.

'OK, Zaid. What does the Arabic word *tawaffa* mean?'

'It means, "He died",' replied Zaid.

'So if I said, "*Abi tawaffa*", it would mean, "my father had died". Correct?'

'Yes, that is what it means.' Then he added, 'May Allah have mercy on him.'

'May he have mercy on us all,' replied Tom, using the standard Arabic formula in response to this statement. Then he went on, 'Now, that word *tawaffa* is used twice of Jesus in the Qur'an. Firstly, it is a statement of Allah about what he is going to do. Allah said to Jesus, "O Jesus, I am going to cause you to die, *mutawaffik*, and raise you to myself."[6] This was the promise of God the Father to Jesus before he was crucified. And Jesus said to Allah, his heavenly Father, "You caused me to die."[7] *Tawaffaytani*. It is the same word.'

'So why does the Qur'an say that "they did not kill him nor crucify him, but it appeared so to them"?'[8] asked Zaid.

'Perhaps this is a response to the dilemma about divine sovereignty and human responsibility. Christians, like Muslims, believe that God is in control of his universe, and this takes into account every event that takes place in history. We also believe that people have freedom, make choices and carry out actions. But God can still fulfil his purposes through our actions, even our sinful actions. Despite the human involvement in and responsibility for the death of Jesus, it is presented as part of the divine plan. Jesus said to his disciples after he rose from the dead, "Everything must be fulfilled that is written about me in the Law of Moses, the Prophets and the Psalms ... This is what is written: The Messiah will suffer and rise from the dead on the third day".[9] That Jesus was crucified by Roman soldiers at the instigation of the Jewish leaders was God working out his eternal purposes through a human agency.

---

[5] Q 19.33.

[6] Q 3.55.

[7] Q 5.117.

[8] Q 4.157.

[9] Luke 24:44–45.

'In a similar way, the remarkable victory at Badr when Muslim soldiers defeated an army of Meccan idolaters three times their number is presented as the direct physical action of God. The Holy Qur'an says, "You did not kill them [the Meccans] but Allah killed them. And when you threw [rocks, spears, arrows], you did not throw, but Allah threw".[10] So, people can act freely and they must take responsibility for their actions, but God still carries out his ultimate plan by means of their actions. Jesus' death on the cross, like the Muslim victory at Badr, was a part of God's sovereign purposes.'

The audience, who had begun buzzing when Zaid stood up, now became silent when they heard this comparison. Zaid, still on his feet, took advantage of the silence, 'But Jesus dying for the sins of others does not make sense. Why would the death of an innocent person be necessary? And why would an innocent one die for a guilty one anyway?'

Tom took a deep breath. 'Those are two very good questions, and they need two different answers. Let me deal with them by telling a story.'

The audience almost as one leaned forward in their seats. Tom also leaned forward – he now had the initiative. 'There were once two brothers who looked very much alike, so much so that people thought they were identical twins. But there was a year's difference in age between them and that was not the only difference. They contrasted completely in character. The older brother was hardworking and well-behaved – everyone who knew him loved and respected him. But the younger brother was the opposite. He was lazy, a liar and a violent drunkard.

---

10 Q 8.17.

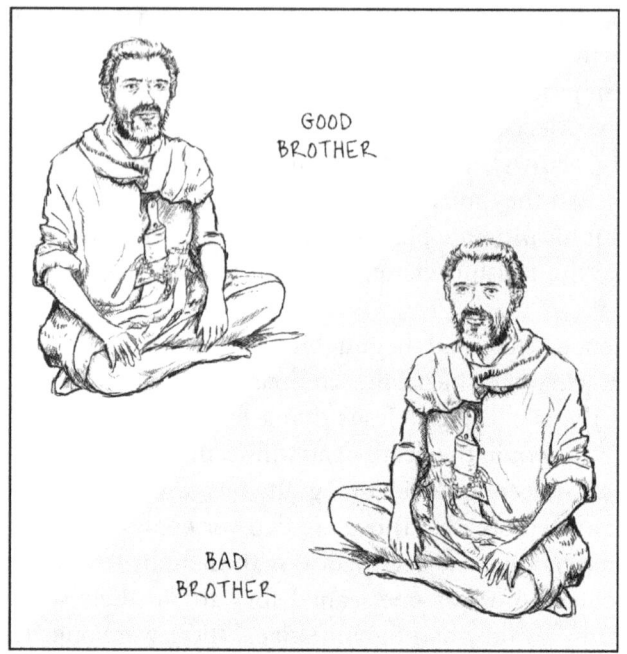

GOOD
BROTHER

BAD
BROTHER

THEY LOOKED LIKE TWINS,
BUT THEY DIFFERED IN CHARACTER.

'One day, the younger brother got into a fight in the marketplace. He pulled out a knife and killed his opponent.'

The students showed no surprise at this event. Every Yemeni man, as a part of their national dress, wears a large curved *jambiya* on his belt, and these knives are often used in street fights.

Tom continued, 'The relatives of the dead man began to pursue the younger brother. But he could run fast. He raced to the house of his older brother, still carrying the bloodied *jambiya*, and with bloodstains on his white *thobe*. He knocked loudly on his brother's door. The older brother opened up the door, looked at him and saw the pursuing crowd in the distance. He immediately realised what had happened and he knew what he must do. He pulled his brother inside, locked the door and said, "I can save you, but you must do what I tell you."

THE MOMENT OF SALVATION.

'The younger brother nodded in agreement. "Firstly, take off your *thobe* and put on my clean *thobe*." They exchanged clothes. Then the older brother said, "Now, give me the knife." The younger brother handed it over.

'Just then, the relatives of the slain man arrived, looking for the murderer. They began hammering on the door. As they did so, the older brother opened the door and walked out to face them, but he did not say a word. Seeing him holding the bloodied *jambiya* and wearing clothes with blood on them, they assumed he was the killer, and they set upon him with their own *jambiyas* and killed him on the spot.

'The younger brother saw this through the open door and was overcome with guilt. He immediately ran outside and shouted, "Stop! You have killed the wrong man. He was innocent. I am the guilty one."

'A great discussion arose in the crowd over which brother had committed the crime – some said that they had killed the murderer, but others thought the younger brother was the guilty one. Most could not tell the difference between the two. Then cooler heads in the mob began to prevail. They discussed what should be done.

'In the centre of the town was a wise judge, so they set off to the court, with two men holding the arms of the younger brother, who was crying, and others carrying the two dead men on makeshift stretchers. The judge listened carefully to everyone, including the younger brother who, having seen his brother killed, was now extremely repentant. Then, the wise judge gave his verdict. He said to them, "You all know that we practice the law of *intaqaam*, retributive revenge, in our community. If someone kills a member of your family, you have the right to kill any member of their family. A life for a life. The holy Qur'an teaches that.[11] And that's what has happened today."

'The judge turned to the relatives of the man killed in the marketplace and pointed to the younger brother. "This man killed one of your relatives, and you have carried out your revenge on his older brother. So the debt is now paid. You can do nothing else. You must not take any further action."

'The judge then turned to the younger brother, "You are a lucky man. Your brother paid the price of your crime by his death, so you are free to go now; your safety is guaranteed. But you have to live the rest of your life knowing that someone died in your place so that you might live. Go and live a good life."

'From that day, the younger brother was a changed person. He gave up his life of laziness, lying, drinking and violence. He became a hardworking and honest man, serving others, and eventually, he won the respect and love of all the people of his village.'

Tom turned to Zaid, 'So, the story answers both your questions, Zaid. God is a just judge. No wrongdoing will ultimately go unpunished. Every sin requires retribution – someone has to pay for it. And, secondly, an innocent person, out of love for a guilty one, may choose to pay the price for that sinner, even if it costs an innocent life.'

---

11 Q 5.45.

'But isn't that unjust?' It was Zaid again. 'Isn't it unfair for an innocent one to suffer for a guilty person? Where is the equity in that?'

Tom paused for a moment and then said, 'There is a story in the Hadith about the prophet, Muhammad.'

At the mention of his name, the audience responded in unison, '*Sall Allah 'alayhi wa sallam*' (Prayers and peace from Allah be upon him).

'Actually, there are ten different versions of this story in *Sahih al-Bukhari*,[12] so I will give you a combined version. It was Ramadan, and a man came to the Prophet with a confession. He said, "O Prophet of Allah, I have sinned. I had sexual relations with my wife during the daylight hours."

'As you know, every person must abstain from food, drink and sex during the daytime. The Prophet asked, "Can you set free a slave as expiation?" The man said he couldn't. The Prophet said, "Can you fast for two months?" The man said he couldn't. The Prophet asked, "Can you feed sixty poor persons?" The man said, "No".

'Just then, a basket of dates was brought for the Prophet to break his fast. He gave it to the man and said, "Take this and give it in charity."

'The man said, "Should I give it to a poorer family than mine? I know of no family in Medina which is poorer than my family."

'At that, the Prophet smiled and said, "Feed your family with it." And the man went away happily with the basket of dates.'[13]

Tom again turned to Zaid, 'So Zaid, in this story, who sinned: the man or the Prophet?'

'The man, of course,' responded Zaid.

Tom asked, 'And who paid the price for the sin: the man who sinned or the Prophet?'

The significance of this hit home. Zaid lowered his voice: 'The Prophet.'

'This is just a simple instance of an innocent person paying for the sin of a guilty one,' said Tom. 'The innocent person gives up something they were entitled to, while the guilty one receives the benefit when in fact, they deserved punishment. That is an example from the life of the Prophet.'

---

12 *Sahih al-Bukhari* 3.156–158, 772; 7.281; 8.110, 185, 700, 701, 702; 8.111.1, 111.2. There are many collections of the Hadith or traditions about Muhammad. *Sahih al-Bukhari* is the most respected of them, followed by *Sahih Muslim*. They can be found on the website sunnah.com

13 *Sahih al-Bukhari* 1935, 1936, 1937, 5368, etc., https://sunnah.com/bukhari:1936

At this, the whole audience burst into applause. They loved to hear these positive stories about their Prophet.

But Tom pressed home his point. 'This helps to understand why Jesus died. He was innocent, and we are guilty. He gave up his life so that we could live. That is basically what Christianity is all about. It's about God's love, God's grace and God's forgiveness.'

At this, Ali decided it was time to end the meeting. He stood up and thanked Tom for speaking to the group and said they would like to invite him back.

After some polite applause, the students filed out, some stopping to shake his hand and thank him personally. The last one to leave was a young man with intense eyes. He had been hanging back, waiting for the others to leave. 'I would really like to talk more with you about this. Could you come to my house? Here's my address.' He handed Tom a piece of paper.

'Sure. I would love to do that. When?' asked Tom.

'How about Friday after prayers?'

'Great. What's your name?'

'Mahmoud,' replied the student. 'I'll see you on Friday.' And he walked off quickly.

9. Three In One

Mahmoud blew a column of cigarette smoke upwards and leaned back. He and Tom were in the *majlis* (sitting room) in Mahmoud's house, which was just around the corner from Tom and Hannah's apartment. Tom had been visiting him every Friday afternoon for several weeks now. Mahmoud had been at the mosque for the compulsory noon prayers and the weekly sermon, and he was in the mood to discuss theology.

'The imam talked about Christians today,' he said. 'He told us that they can't count.'

Tom rolled his eyes. 'Why did he say that?'

'He said that they claim to believe in one God, but they actually have three – God the father, God the mother and God the son.[1] He said that three can't be one, and one can't be three. So they can't count. You don't believe in three gods, do you?'

'No,' said Tom. 'Your imam seems a bit confused.' He knew he was on safe ground because Mahmoud had often mocked the imam. Even though he led the congregation, the imam was, according to Mahmoud, an illiterate country hick. 'God the mother has never been considered part of the Trinity.'

'Even I knew that,' Mahmoud replied. 'He is such an idiot. But tell me about the three and the one. One plus one plus one always equals three, doesn't it?'

'Yes, it does,' said Tom. 'How old were you when you learned that, Mahmoud?'

'About five or six years old. In Grade One in my village school.'

'Was that the only mathematical equation you learned at school?' asked Tom.

'No, we learned lots of things – addition, subtraction, multiplication, division, fractions …'

---

1 Q 5.116.

'OK, let's do some multiplication. If I multiply one by one by one, that is three ones, what do I get?' Tom held up three fingers on his left hand, counting off the 'ones' as he spoke.

'That's easy – one times one times one equals one.'

Tom held up one finger on his right hand. 'So three can be one,' said Tom, bringing his two hands together. 'That's Grade Three mathematics.'

Mahmoud laughed. 'Perhaps my imam never got that far in school.'

Tom continued. 'Look at this room. It has a length, a width and a height. How many dimensions are here?'

'Three.'

'And how many rooms are we in?' asked Tom.

'Just one,' replied Mahmoud. 'Hmm. I can see what you are getting at – being three and one at the same time is not impossible.'

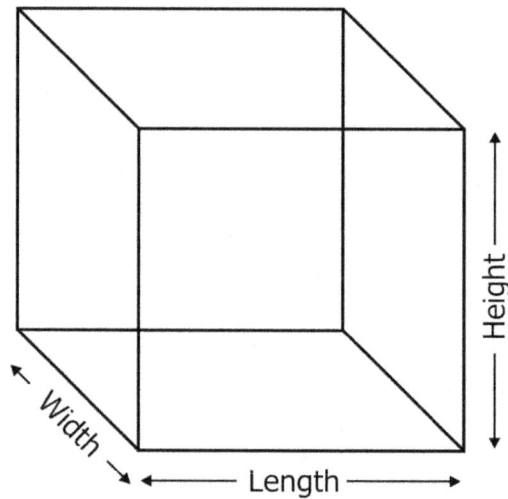

BEING THREE AND ONE AT THE SAME TIME
IS NOT IMPOSSIBLE.

'Thank you, Professor Mahmoud,' said Tom. 'So, how is that different from the Muslim view of Allah?' He asked rhetorically.

'Let me show you something,' said Tom. He took a piece of paper from his shirt pocket. On the top of it he wrote in capital letters 'GOD IS ONE'.

'I agree with that,' said Mahmoud. 'We Muslims believe in *tawheed*, the unity of Allah, but you Christians believe in the Trinity. And Trinity is not even in the Bible. How can you believe in something that is not in your holy book?'

'That's a very good point,' replied Tom. 'So, if a word is not in my holy book, I shouldn't believe it?'

'Of course not,' said Mahmoud triumphantly. 'It is just a word made up by a person.'

'But I have read the Qur'an in Arabic, and the Hadith in Arabic, and the word *tawheed* does not appear in either of them. Check for yourself or ask your imam. So, you shouldn't believe in the unity of Allah either ... *touché.*' Mahmoud had a French-speaking Lebanese girlfriend once, so he understood this term.

'OK, please continue with your drawing.'

Tom went on. 'Christians and Muslims both believe in God's unity,' and he wrote 'unity' underneath. 'But there are two types of unity: one is a *simple* unity.'

'All unity is simple,' said Mahmoud.' You can't get simpler than "one".'

'We will see,' said Tom. 'Some examples of a simple unity would be a "point" or "dot" in geometry, because it exists in only one dimension.' He drew a dot and labelled it.

'What thing in biology has only one cell?' he asked Mahmoud.

'Some kind of virus or microbe?'

'Right. For example, an amoeba. It is a single-celled organism. You can't get simpler than that.'

'But you can get very sick from an amoeba. Don't ever eat at Abdullah's cafe on the corner. It's full of them.'

'So, a simple unity is not always healthy? We'll come back to that,' said Tom, raising his eyebrows, while drawing and labelling an amoeba.

'Hey, you're up to something. I can tell,' said Mahmoud.

Tom went on. 'A simple unity in sociology would be a lone human being, because it has a single centre of consciousness.' He drew a human stick figure.

'And when Muslims talk about Allah, they describe him as a simple unity, because there can be no division or separation in his *dhat* or essential nature.' Tom drew a circle with 'Allah' written inside.

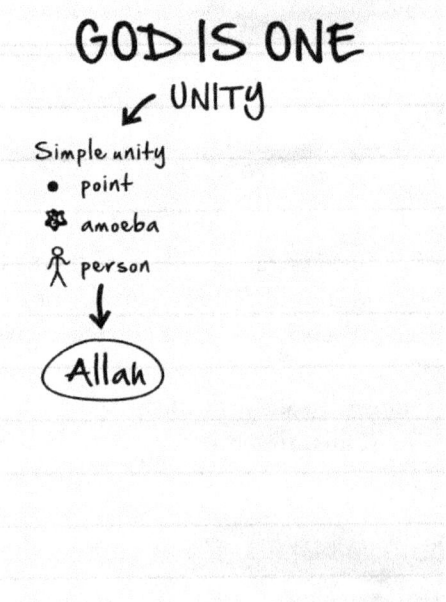

'That's true,' said Mahmoud. 'Our sheikh said that even Allah's characteristics, his *sifaat*, are separate from his *dhat*, otherwise that might jeopardise his unity. Allah is indivisible. He is one!' He spoke this last bit triumphantly.

Tom went on. 'And this impacts the way that you pray as Muslims. You must pray facing one direction, to Mecca, in one language, Arabic, using the same set of actions or *rakahs*, and at the same timetable each day. So Islam tends to uniformity, one way of doing things, and conformity, everyone must do them.' He drew a small diagram of a prostrating man and wrote these last few terms.

'Yes! That is our strength in Islam. If we would all follow the way or *sunna* of Muhammad, we Muslims would be united, and then,' he smiled wickedly, winking, 'we could easily defeat the *kafir*, infidels, like you.'

Tom ignored this geopolitical supremacist sentiment, certain that Mahmoud did not believe it. He was simply repeating a sentiment that was shouted out by the imam from the mosque's loudspeaker each Friday.

Tom commented, 'The reason Muslims pray the same way without variation every day is a reflection of the kind of God you worship. Allah is a simple unity, with no internal differentiation or variety.'

'Yes, I agree with that,' said Mahmoud. 'But don't you believe in the same thing? We all worship the same God, don't we?'

'We'll see.' He drew a line down the middle of the page. 'Let's look at another kind of "unity",' Tom said. He wrote 'complex unity' on the right-hand side. Under it, and opposite the drawings of the point, amoeba and person, he drew a cube, a human body, and a group of circles inside a circle.

'These are examples of complex unities in geometry, biology and sociology. Each of them is a unity, but several entities make up that unity. A cube has three dimensions, but it is a single shape. A human body has many differentiated and specialised cells, but it is one living organism. And a group of people, such as a family or team or nation, consists of many individuals who differ from each other but have some characteristics in common. *E pluribus unum* (From the many, one). It is unity in diversity, a complex unity.'

'Hmm.' Mahmoud was interested in these contrasts.

Tom then drew a heart with three circles inside. 'As Christians, we are told that "God is love".[2] We are also told that God is the Father, Son and Holy Spirit.'

This was too much for Mahmoud. 'That is what the apostle Paul taught when he invented the Trinity.'

'Actually, that's not true!' replied Tom. 'Jesus said, "Baptise in the name, singular, of the Father and of the Son and of the Holy Spirit".[3] Jesus spoke this long before Paul even became a Christian.'

'Is that true?' asked Mahmoud.

'You can check it yourself. What is important is that, if God is love, then there had to be more than a simple unity right from the beginning.'

'What do you mean?'

Tom said, 'Love always requires an object. You can't just "love". Love must have an object – you have to love somebody or something.'

'Everyone knows that!' replied Mahmoud.

Tom asked, 'Who did Allah love before the world was created?'

Mahmoud frowned. 'I've never thought about that.'

Tom continued, 'A being who is totally and eternally alone is a lonely being, with no-one to relate to and no ability to do so. With the Trinity, this problem is overcome – love is exhibited between the Three Persons even if no-one or nothing else exists. Jesus said to his heavenly Father, "You loved me before the creation of the world".[4] Jesus existed before the world was created.'

'What about the Holy Spirit?' asked Mahmoud.

'The second verse of the Bible, Genesis 1:2, tells us that the Spirit of God was hovering over the waters as the world was being created. The Spirit was clearly present before the world began. All three divine Persons existed together from eternity. Consequently, the Christian understanding of God leads to variety and freedom in worship.'

---

2 1 John 4:8–16.

3 Matt 28:19.

4 John 17:24.

'Why do you say that?' asked Mahmoud.

'There is variety, because we find that there is distinction and differentiation even within the nature of God himself. The Father is not the Son; the Son is not the Spirit; the Spirit is not the Father. So, Christian worship allows us to express that variety in the ways we worship – there is no set direction for prayer, no required language, no specified times, no mandated method. That gives Christians great freedom to express themselves.'

Tom wrote these into the diagram, along with the words 'variety' and 'freedom'.

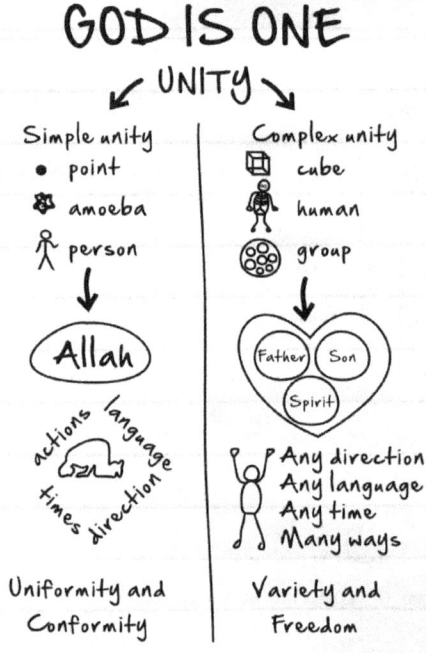

'That makes sense,' said Mahmoud. 'But so what? Besides liberty and diversity in worship for Christians, does the idea of the Trinity have any practical value? I can see that the Trinity may be explainable, but that does not mean that it is useful. Does understanding God as three-in-one deliver any concrete outcomes?'

'Actually', said Tom, 'the Trinity is the most practical doctrine that has ever been revealed. Let me tell you a story.'

Mahmoud stubbed his cigarette on the concrete windowsill. He flicked the butt out the window through a small hole in the wire screen, then sat up and concentrated. He loved Tom's stories.

Tom began, 'One night, there was a man named Ahmed, walking through the desert. It was very dark, and unfortunately Ahmed fell into a deep and narrow pit in the sand. Try as he might, he could not get out because the sides of the hole were sheer and the sand was very soft. In fact, the more he tried, the more the sand flowed down around him and the worse his situation got. Soon, he was buried up to his waist, and he couldn't move.

'He realised that he would never escape without some help. Desperate, he called out. (Tom cupped his hands to his mouth and yelled upwards) "Help. If there's anybody up there, please come and help me!"

'Soon, a face appeared at the top of the hole. The person said, "I can see you are in very great trouble. I would love to come down and help you, but I cannot because I am by myself – I am all alone. But I will send you down a book, and perhaps you can work out how to save yourself." He dropped a book down to Ahmed, and then, he disappeared.'

'Mahmoud was unhappy with this solution. 'Huh! A book! What good would that be?'

Tom went on, lowering his voice. 'Meanwhile, on the same night in another part of the desert, a man named Mabruuk was walking by himself. And he also fell into a deep hole – there were lots of holes in this desert. Mabruuk also struggled to get out, and quickly became buried up to his waist in the sand. He called out. "Help. If there's anybody up there, please come and help me!"

'Soon, three faces appeared at the top of the hole and looked down. One of them said: "We can see that you are in a very difficult situation. But don't worry! We will work together to save you."

'Of the three, one was very strong – he could lift anything. He said, "I have a long rope with me. If someone is willing to go, I will lower him down into the hole."

'Of the three, one was very brave – he would go anywhere and try anything. He said, "I am willing. I will go down to save Mabruuk."'

'The third one was very gentle – he would help anyone. He said, "I will help my strong friend hold the rope."'

'And so they began. The brave one took the rope and tied it around his waist. The strong one and the gentle one lowered him into the hole, very slowly because the walls were unstable. The brave one arrived at the bottom. He carefully dug Mabruuk out of the soft sand. He took the rope off himself and tied it around Mabruuk's waist. The two above began to pull Mabruuk to safety. But, just as he got to the top, Mabruuk's foot hit the side of the hole and all of the sand collapsed onto the brave one ten metres below, and he died.'

This was too much for Mahmoud. 'Oh no!' he cried out. 'What a tragedy! The brave one tried to save someone else and he died himself.'

Tom stopped him. 'But listen, there's more. That's not the end of the story. The strong one and the gentle one said, 'Even though our companion is dead, we will not abandon him in the desert.'

'And they dug and they dug in the soft sand for three whole days. Eventually, they found the body of the brave one. Mabruuk wept aloud at the sight, but the gentle one said, "Don't weep. I can breathe into him, and by the power of God, he will come back to life again."'

'And he leaned over and breathed and breathed, and soon the brave one came back to life. And there was great rejoicing. Not only had the brave hero come to life, but Mabruuk, who had been lost, was saved.'

Tom then turned to Mahmoud. 'So, my brother, who would you like to be in this story? Ahmed who is still trying to save himself by reading his book? Or Mabruuk who was saved by the death of the brave one who came to his rescue?'

Mahmoud laughed. 'You are very clever, Tom. Of course I want to be Mabruuk.'

Tom explained to him, 'You know what we Christians believe. In the Trinity, we have a loving Father in heaven. He is God who is *for* us. He sent his Son Jesus Christ into the world to save us, and in the process, Jesus died and then rose again. Jesus is Immanuel, God who is *with* us. Then, the Father and the Son sent the Holy Spirit who comes to live in our hearts and transform our lives. The Spirit is God *in* us. All three Persons work together to save us.'

HELP AT LAST!

'I am beginning to understand the ideas,' said Mahmoud, 'and that *is* a gripping story.'

'Thanks,' said Tom, standing up. 'Anyway, I'd better go. I am teaching the day after tomorrow, and I have a lecture to prepare.'

Mahmoud stood up and embraced him. '*Inshallah*, it will go well. You are a good teacher.'

As Tom walked home in the warm evening, he prayed.

10. A Shameful Display

Thump! A large rock hit the wooden shutters protecting the glass window beside Tom's head as he sat at home preparing his lecture. Tom got up from his desk and ran to the front door. He went out to the tin gate, slid back the large metal bolt and opened it. No-one was there. This was the fourth time this week. Always at 3 pm. He suspected the local kids, on their way home from school. There had also been the rocks thrown over their wall into their back courtyard. One had narrowly missed Hannah as she was hanging out the washing. It was becoming a pattern. It was starting to wear thin. So Tom set a trap.

The next day at 3pm, he was sitting in their back courtyard reading a book when he heard a loud thump in the front courtyard, followed by footsteps running down the side lane behind their house. He quickly stepped out the back gate and managed to grab the third of three boys who were running past. Their loud laughter turned to cries of dismay. The two older boys ran into a nearby lane. Holding the smaller one by the scruff of the neck, Tom raced after them.

As they ran around a corner, Tom was right behind them. But he stopped suddenly. The narrow, abandoned alleys gave way to a large square, filled with many people. The two boys ahead of him suddenly stopped and turned, pointing to Tom and the boy he was holding. They began shouting in Arabic. The crowd went quiet, and some started walking towards Tom. The boy that he was holding suddenly started squirming, trying to escape from Tom's grip. He responded by squeezing harder on the boy's neck, and the boy dropped to the ground, screaming aloud and thrashing about. A large man with a machine gun hanging over his shoulder came up to Tom and shouted, 'What are you doing?'

'Who is the father of this boy? He has been throwing rocks at my house every day,' yelled Tom in reply.

'Let him go. You're hurting him,' shouted the man.

'Yes, let him go,' said others from the square, who were now gathered around Tom and the boy. 'He didn't do anything. He's just a kid.'

Tom realised that he was in a tricky situation. The mob was getting larger and angrier. The boy, sensing that the event had turned in his favour, screamed even louder.

'I'm not letting him go until his father comes!' shouted Tom, partly from anger, partly from fear. He thought to himself, *What's going to happen here? I can't just let him go or the rocks will just keep coming, maybe even get worse. How am I going to get out of this?*

Tom's salvation came in a most unusual form. A small woman, completely enveloped in a black burqa, ran out of a nearby house and hit him on the head with a wooden broom handle.

This caught Tom by surprise and he let go of the boy. Fortunately for him, as it turned out, the blow split the skin on his forehead and blood began to flow freely down his face. Realising his situation had just improved, Tom grabbed his head, fell to the ground, lay still and groaned.

The sight of the foreigner lying on the ground, bleeding and groaning, turned the tide of sympathy in the opposite direction. Two men immediately picked Tom up and half-walked, half-carried him back to his house. 'It will be all right, it will be all right,' they kept saying.

Hannah met Tom as he came in. She was exasperated at his inability to control his anger. 'It will get you into trouble,' she scolded him as she put a dressing on the wound. At least it didn't need stitches.

Within an hour, there was a knock at the door. Yousef and Umar from next door were standing there with a man and woman.

'This is Abdul Kareem, the father of the boy you, er … captured,' said Yousef.

'And this is Amina, his mother. She hit you on the head with the stick,' said Umar. 'They have come to say they are sorry and to ask that you not inform the police.' Yemeni police had a particularly bad reputation and were said to even torture those who were reported to them to extort money from them.

'Of course, I won't tell the police,' said Tom. 'It was my fault. I lost my temper.'

'But they would like to invite you to dinner tonight, to mend the relationship. Could you come at 9pm, you and your wife?' asked Yousef.

'We would love to come,' said Tom, looking at Hannah, who was nodding.

That evening, Tom and Hannah walked hand-in-hand to Abdul Kareem and Amina's house. Unlike many other Arabs, Yemeni husbands and wives did walk hand-in-hand, but usually only when crossing the road together. Tom and Hannah decided to expand the geographical borders of this custom. They came up to the house where Amina had run out from that afternoon. Tom shivered as he remembered the events of the day. *God can redeem anything,* he thought to himself, *even the results of my stupidity.* They had prayed before they left home that this would be an opportunity to share some truth.

The house was a typical Yemeni dwelling, surrounded by a high concrete wall with broken glass embedded on top to deter thieves. The tin gate was noisy when Abdul Kareem opened it, and he greeted them warmly. Tom and Hannah entered the small front courtyard. It was paved with concrete, and several small, broken bicycles were leaning against its walls. The courtyard was dark, but the multicoloured kaleidoscope of a *qamariya,* a semi-circular stained-glass window above the front door, beckoned. They went inside after removing their shoes. Hannah was immediately whisked away to another room by Amina and her teenage daughter, who was a full head taller than her mother. In most Yemeni households, the women eat separately from the men when visitors come.

Abdul Kareem led Tom upstairs to the *mafraj,* a special room for male gatherings. There was a series of long, narrow, brightly coloured, mattress-like couches against the walls on every side. Abdul Kareem sat down and gestured to Tom to sit beside him. Tom lowered himself into this floor-couch. The room smelled of cigarette smoke and incense and perfume. Abdul Kareem lit up a cigarette.

'I am so sorry for what my son has been doing to you. He has brought great shame on our family. I gave him a severe beating this afternoon.'

Tom immediately felt guilty. 'No, it was my fault,' he said. 'I should have dealt with it differently. I did not want to shame you. Honour is very important in your community. I am the one who should feel ashamed.'

'OK, let's call it even,' smiled Abdul Kareem, reaching over and putting his hand on Tom's knee, squeezing it. Tom was now used to such physical displays of affection among men and took it as it was meant.

Just then, Amina and her daughter brought in the food. They placed the huge tray on the floor in front of them. It held a sea of rice with an island of mutton in the middle, and salad dotted around the edges.

'*Bismillah*,' said Abdul Kareem, invoking the name of Allah. They began to eat, using just their hands, plunging into the rice and flicking it gently into their mouths. This was a messy but satisfying way to eat.

As they ate, Tom returned to the earlier topic. 'We were talking about shame and honour before. I have a story about that. Would you like to hear it?'

'Of course,' said Abdul Kareem. 'Everybody loves to hear stories, especially if they have a deeper meaning.'

'Well, you can tell me what you think the meaning of this story is. It is about a young man who was conscripted into the army and sent off to fight for his country in a war.'

'This is not just a story,' interrupted Abdul Kareem. 'It is a reality. Every young man in this country has to serve in the army, and we have had so many wars. Many of my companions were killed or injured when they served in the army.'

'Well, this young man was fortunate,' continued Tom. 'After two years, he returned home safely. His family was overjoyed. His mother said, "I have cooked your favourite meal, with meat and chicken and *hilbah* and *bint al-sahn*. Come and eat."

'The young man replied, "In the army, I learnt to collect and cook all kinds of insects. It is rough food and not very tasty, but I must rely on myself. I will prepare my own food." His mother felt deflated because of this.

'But then, his sister came to him and said, "Your clothes are dirty and torn. I have spent months making you a new suit from the finest materials I could buy to honour your safe return, and to make you look good."

'The young man replied, "I have worn this army uniform for the past two years and it has served me well. I know how to patch it, so I will continue to wear it." The sister felt rejected. All her hard work was wasted.

'Then, the young man's father came to him and said, "I have built a new room onto the house for you. It is beautifully decorated with the best furnishings we could afford. Now, you can marry any girl you want and bring her here to live. Come and see your new room."

'But the young man replied, "In the army, we learned how to make rough shelters from some plastic sheeting and sticks and rocks. I will make a dwelling like that and live in it. I must rely on myself." The father felt disregarded.

'The next day, the people from the village came to welcome the son who had returned from the army. But, when they arrived at the house, they saw a young man in torn and dirty clothes in a field beside the house. He was living in a rough shelter, collecting and cooking insects. Some thought that he was a beggar, or a farm labourer. They asked the father where the newly returned son was, and he pointed to the young man living in the field.

"What? Have you no shame? Why did you treat your son like this?"

'The father replied, "We didn't treat him like this. It was his own choice." And the father showed them the food, clothing and room they had prepared for his son and heir.

'When the visitors heard this, they felt great shame for his family. "What son would treat his family like this?" they asked. And they went away sad.'

BOTH THE FAMILY AND THE COMMUNITY FELT ASHAMED
BECAUSE OF THE SON.

Tom stopped. 'So that was my story. What do you think it means?'

Abdul Kareem frowned deeply. 'That is a terrible story. What son would ever do this? I can't imagine that ever happening. But you told the story. You must know what it means.'

'Yes, I do,' said Tom. 'It is a spiritual story about our relationship with God. According to our holy book, God has prepared a great salvation for us.[1] It is said, "What no eye has seen, what no ear has heard, and what no human mind has conceived these are the things God has prepared for those who love him."[2]

'Yes, I know that saying,' said Abdul Kareem. 'It is in our Hadith. It is a saying of our Prophet Muhammad, peace and blessings be upon him.'[3]

Tom knew that there was a lot of borrowing in the Hadith from biblical material, but thought it would be a distraction to mention this. So he went on.

'In the holy Bible, it says that the kingdom God promises us is like a great feast,[4] where we are given new clothes,[5] and can live in a house that is like a mansion.[6] These are all gifts from him. But it is a tragedy that many, like the young returned soldier, would prefer to provide for themselves, by relying on their own good works. These attempts are like filthy rags in God's sight.[7] Those who depend on their own efforts will find themselves despised and rejected and ashamed.'

'But, if we cannot do good works, then what can we do to earn Allah's favour?' asked Abdul Kareem.

'Perhaps we don't need to,' replied Tom. 'The father, mother and sister in that story already loved and accepted their son and brother. He didn't need to do anything else to earn their favour. He simply needed to accept what they had prepared for him.'

This was a radical idea for Abdul Kareem. 'But how are we to do this?' he asked.

---

1 Matt 25:34.

2 1 Cor 2:9.

3 *Sahih al-Bukhari*, https://sunnah.com/bukhari:7498

4 Matt 22:2.

5 Rev 3:18.

6 John 14:2.

7 Isa 64:6.

'It is quite simple and yet very profound,' said Tom. 'For a start, we need to put aside our pride and self-sufficiency and accept the gracious provision that God has made for us. It is only then that we can live the life that he requires of us. Then, we can look forward to the position of honour and dignity that he has planned for us after we die. Jesus, God's Son, said that he has gone to prepare that place for us. One day, he will return to take us to that seat of honour. The question each of us must ask is: Am I willing to go with him?'

Just then, a silver tray of coffee and sweets arrived. This was a sign that the evening was drawing to a close.

Downstairs, the women had also been having a discussion about the same topic of shame and honour.

Amina broached the issue, 'I am so sorry that I hit your husband,' she said to Hannah. 'I just became angry when I saw him holding my son. I knew that my son had done something wrong – he is always getting into trouble at school. But, to see this happening in front of all the neighbours was too much for me.'

'That's OK,' said Hannah. 'I'm sure my husband was not without fault in this. And we all have things that we are ashamed of.'

'Yes, we do,' agreed Amina, 'but what can we do to get rid of that shame?'

'I have a story about that very issue,' said Hannah. 'Would you like to hear it?'

'Of course,' said Amina, relaxing.

Hannah began. 'There was once a powerful king who lived in a luxurious palace. He married a beautiful queen, and they had a lovely son, who grew into a fine young man.

'The king and queen were very happy. The kingdom was prosperous, and all its citizens lived in peace and security. One day, the king looked from his palace into the town below and saw a family begging in the streets. They were dirty, wore ragged clothes and their children were naked. *This is not right*, thought the king. *My kingdom is just and prosperous. There should be no such poverty here.* So the king sent a soldier to find out who these people were.

'The soldier returned and informed the king that they had come as refugees from a far land, where there was war and famine. The king felt pity for the family. He told the soldier, "Take some food and clean clothing from the royal treasury. And grant them some crown land beside the river, good land so they can grow crops and support themselves. But tell them that they will have to pay ten per cent tax on all their produce every year, just like other citizens, to support our capital works program." The soldier went to those people, and they gratefully accepted the food, clothes and land, and agreed to the conditions.'

'What a wonderful king,' interrupted Amina. 'If only we had political leaders who were so generous, wise and just.'

Hannah continued, 'This refugee family began to work hard. They built a small house on the land and planted crops. The land was very good and it produced a fine harvest. This new life was very good.

'At the end of the year, the king sent his servants to collect the taxes throughout the land.

But the refugee family said, "This is our first year, and we do not have much to spare. We will pay next year." The king agreed to this.

'The next year brought a good harvest with a bumper crop. Everyone had more than enough to spare. At the end of the year, the king sent his servants to collect the taxes throughout the land. But the refugee family again refused. They said disrespectfully, "If the king wants crops, he can grow his own."

'When the king heard this, he ignored the insult and sent his Minister of Finance to explain how the tax was going to be spent. But, when the Minister came, this family beat him up, and sent him away. The king said, "OK, I will send my son, my only son, to talk with them. Surely they will respect the prince.'

'When they saw the prince coming, the family said to each other, "This is the heir of the kingdom. If we kill him, we will inherit this land for ourselves." When the prince stepped onto their property, they grabbed him and beat him to death with rocks and sticks. Then, they threw his body outside their front gate.

'The people of that town were horrified at this, and they took the body of the young prince up to the palace and laid it before the king. The king was so angry! He called his general of his army and said, "Collect every weapon you can, call every soldier back from leave, take every piece of artillery you can find, and go down to that house. Destroy it and kill those wicked people."

'But the queen had a different approach. She ordered that the body of the prince be brought into her inner chamber, and she locked the door. She had magical powers that no-one knew about, and she drew upon them to bring the prince back to life. The prince immediately knew what he had to do. He climbed through a trapdoor hidden in the floor of her room and began to run through an underground tunnel.'

'This is such an exciting story!' exclaimed Amina. 'Where is the prince going? What is going to happen?'

'Well, the king's army soon arrived at the refugees' house and surrounded it. The general was about to give the order to attack, but before he could do so, the door of the refugees' house opened and, to everyone's amazement, out walked the now-alive prince. The secret tunnel had taken him to this house. He was followed out by the refugee family. The prince said to the general, "Do not attack. This family is begging for mercy and I have agreed to be their mediator."

'Accompanied by the refugee family and the king's army, the prince walked back up to the palace. He stood before the king and said, "Father, this family is truly sorry for what they have done. They know that it was wrong. They have repented. I want you to spare their lives."

'The king replied, "But they have abused our hospitality, dishonoured my name and brought shame to our land. What will remove this shame?"

'The prince replied, "As you know, we have a saying in our country: 'Nothing removes shame except blood.' My blood lies on the ground outside their house. Will you accept my blood as a payment, to wash away their shame? I have forgiven them for what they did to me."

'The king stood up and declared, "If I had heard this from anyone but you, I would not accept it. But because you, my beloved son, are their mediator and your blood has washed away their sin, I will forgive them." The king stopped. Then he went on. "And more than this, I now invite this family to come and live as guests with you and me and the queen in this beautiful palace as part of our family."

'Wow,' said Amina. 'This is unbelievable.'

Hannah concluded, 'So, those who were once poor, now lived in comfort. Those who were once shamed, now were honoured. Those who were once enemies became the king's friends. And as this story travelled around the kingdom, all the people of that land were astounded at the generosity and forgiveness of the king, the skill and wisdom of the queen, and the courage and love of the son.'

RELEASED FROM SHAME.

'That is a beautiful story,' said Amina. 'If only it were true.'

'It is true in a way,' said Hannah. 'There is a God who loves us and gives us all that we need. But we have acted in shameful and destructive ways, rejecting his messengers. So, he sent his only son into the world, and Jesus was killed on a cross. But three days later, he was brought back to life by the power of the Holy Spirit. Jesus is our mediator, and he intercedes for us. He offers us forgiveness and a new start. God invites us to become part of his family, even though all we deserved was judgement and punishment. He takes our public shame and turns it into public honour.'

Just then, they heard the sound of the door of the *majlis* upstairs opening, and the men's footsteps on the stairs. 'It sounds like it is time to go,' said Hannah.

'You have given me much to think about,' said Amina. 'I would love to talk more with you about this.'

At the front door, Abdul Kareem embraced Tom, and Amina hugged Hannah before they left. 'That was so enjoyable. We must do this again,' said Abdul Kareem.

'Yes, we must,' said Tom. 'But you must come to our house. Next week, we are having a party for our *eid,* when we celebrate our biggest yearly event. We are inviting many of our neighbours. Would you like to join us?'

Abdul Kareem and Amina looked at each other. 'Of course,' they said in unison.

Tom and Hannah walked home along the dark streets, holding hands and thanking God for a great evening. But both of them were thinking about next week's party.

11. A Stunning Sacrifice

The night of the party seemed to arrive slowly. Tom and Hannah had spent many hours praying and planning and preparing. They talked through each idea not only with each other, but also with their Yemeni friends, Yousef and Umar next door, and the students, Mahmoud, Ali, Bilal and Khalid. The consensus was that a generous meal should be served, and lots of entertainment provided. Tom and Hannah decided that ordering food from a local, well-respected restaurant would be best, as they had not mastered preparing the local rice and meat dish to any level of acceptability. Hannah invited Amina around to help her cook *bint al-sahn*, a local flaky-pastry cake drenched in honey.

Invitations were sent out to many of the neighbours, both male and female, to some of their colleagues from the university and Hannah's clinic, and to a few of the students. It was an eclectic mix, and Tom and Hannah were not sure how the different groups would view each other and whether they would get along. Everyone who was invited said they would come along *inshallah*, if Allah willed. Tom and Hannah still had no way of knowing whether these were genuine acceptances and intentions or not. The estimate of the number of guests ranged between twenty and one hundred. They decided to cater for seventy, but were ready to order more food from the restaurant after people arrived if necessary.

On the night of the party, the Middle Eastern moon shone brightly. Tom had erected a large tent, rented from a shop that catered for local weddings. The tent was set up on the spacious, flat roof of their house.

People started to arrive. The men went upstairs onto the roof. The women, with a sprinkling of small babies, went into the *majlis*, the large room designed for men's *khat* chewing sessions. Soon, fifty men were sitting around a large fire that was burning on a sheet of tin raised up on bricks. It was winter – a bit chilly, but still pleasant enough. The twenty women seated on the floor around the *majlis* did not need any form of warmth.

In one corner of the roof, Yousef was tuning up a melodious eleven-stringed oud, flanked by Umar and another man gently tapping on a goatskin tabla. Downstairs, the women had electronic music, and the singing and dancing began. Soon, they were shrieking with delight as each woman tried to outdo the others by performing increasingly sensuous body gyrations. The men's dancing was more disciplined and choreographed. Only those who were competent danced; the rest sat and watched, singing and clapping. The dozen or so dancers followed Abdul Kareem, an accomplished dancer. They copied every one of his complex steps, while waving their *jambiyas* in the air. After about half an hour of vigorous dancing, singing and clapping, interest and energy began to wane. It was time for the next activity.

Tom stood up to speak. Like all the other men, he wore a long, white *thobe* and the local headscarf. He said, '*Ahlan wa sahlan ila bayti.*' (Welcome to my home.) They replied in chorus, '*Ahlah bak, ya Docteur Tom* (Welcome to you, O Doctor Tom).'

Tom continued, 'In past days, the Arabs had no TV or radio. They used to gather on nights like these around a fire to tell each other stories.'

'It was better then,' one called out.

'Yes,' said Tom. 'So tonight, we will revive that old tradition.'

The men cheered and clapped. Tom smiled and silently thanked God for this opportunity. He was holding a carved, wooden walking stick with a small, metal axe head attached on the end. This was used by local men when travelling in the mountains. The axe head was a protection against any snakes they might encounter and useful for cutting firewood for their evening campfires. 'Whoever is holding the stick can speak. Who wants to tell the first story?'

Ali jumped to his feet and Tom handed him the stick. He told a story about the Prophet Muhammad and how he had performed a miracle by feeding over forty people from a single plate of mutton. Everyone said, '*alhumdulillah!*'

Unhappy with this pious tale, Yousef seized the stick from Ali and took his opportunity to change the tone. He had been drinking before the event. Tom knew this because he had confiscated a bottle of scotch whiskey from him as he entered. Alcohol was illegal for Yemenis, although easily accessible in the black market, and Tom did not want to give the police any reason to bring a case against him if someone complained. Tom told Yousef, 'This is a *halal* household.'

Yousef got his revenge by telling a very bawdy joke. Tom didn't understand the Arabic – it was too colloquial – but the content was obvious. Most of the men roared with laughter, but the 'ABC' boys sitting in the corner were frowning and mumbling among themselves. Tom felt it was time to intervene.

'I have a story too!' he announced, grabbing the stick from Yousef. This got their attention.

He began. 'Some years ago, my country was invaded by a foreign nation, so I joined the army to defend my nation. We were greatly outnumbered by the invaders. One time, our unit was attacked by the enemy, so we were forced to retreat to a fortress on the top of a hill. The fortress was completely surrounded by the enemy. It was also the headquarters of our army, and our top general was there. He radioed for reinforcements, and other units were on the way to help us. The general gave us strict orders. "No-one is to leave the fortress. This is a place of safety. Going outside is dangerous."

'But I was a young man, and after an hour or so, I got bored. I thought, *The enemy may not be as strong as we think. Perhaps I could go out and sneak through their lines and bring back reinforcements. I will become a hero.* So I sneaked out of the fortress, and began to crawl down the hill. Unfortunately, the enemy soldiers saw me coming and opened fire. A bullet hit me in the leg. I fell to the ground and I could not get up. My leg was broken, and blood was spurting out of the wound. My fellow soldiers saw me from the fortress. They called out, "Get up and run. Save yourself." But I couldn't even stand up, let alone run.

'One soldier threw out an army first-aid manual and it slid down the mountain and stopped beside me. "Read this and treat yourself," he shouted. But I was too wounded to do anything.

'No-one dared to come and help me because of the enemy fire. However, the general of the army also saw me. He knew my situation was dire. He saw the blood flowing from my leg and knew that I would soon bleed to death. He had access to heavy body armour and a powerful gun, but these would slow him down. So he laid them aside in order to move fast. He ran out of the fortress, and down the hill towards me.

'When he arrived, I felt so embarrassed. I said, "Sir, please forgive me. I disobeyed your orders." He said, "Son, I forgive you. But now your safety is the most important issue."

'He was a big, strong man, and he picked me up and began to run up the long hill, carrying me in front of him. The enemy opened fire on us. Three times he was struck by bullets, but he ran on. As we arrived at the gate of the fortress, an enemy mortar bomb exploded behind him. He dropped me at the door of the fortress and fell back dead. His body rolled down the hill and came to rest on the branches of a tree that had been uprooted by the blast. My fellow soldiers grabbed me and dragged me inside. They bound up my wounds and reset my leg.

'From the military hospital bed, I could see the body of the general hanging on the dead tree. I cried and cried, because I knew that his body had protected me from the bullets of the enemy and the mortar blast. He had redeemed my life by sacrificing himself. So, every day I give thanks for the general who gave his life for me.'

THE COURAGEOUS GENERAL GAVE HIS LIFE
FOR A DISOBEDIENT SOLDIER.

There was a deep silence. Some men were wiping tears from their faces. Bilal was looking a bit cynical. He asked, 'Professor Tom – that is a good story. But is it a true story?'

Tom replied, 'Yes, it is a true story, but not an actual historical story. You see, it is a symbolic story – everything in it is a symbol of something that is real.'

'What do you mean?' asked Bilal.

'The war is a symbol of the struggle between us and the devil,' explained Tom. 'Satan has invaded our world with his demons, and the bullets and bombs are like the temptations of Satan that are thrown against us daily. A person living in the fortress is in the centre of God's will, in a place of safety, walking on the straight path. A person who goes outside the fortress is like someone who has disobeyed God. Committing sin leaves one wounded, injured in the heart and soul, unable to help himself. No amount of advice or information will be of benefit. What is needed is someone who will come to do for us what we cannot do for ourselves. The general in this story is like Jesus Christ, who laid aside his heavenly majesty and entered our world to rescue us. The noble Qur'an says that Jesus healed the sick, gave sight to the blind and raised the dead. In other words, he helped everyone who needed it. Despite this, people rejected Christ, and he suffered and died when he sacrificed his life for our sakes. Every day I am grateful that Jesus has rescued me from the devil, from sin and from hell.'

'As Muslims, we do not believe in that,' stated Mahmoud. 'But we are glad to hear your perspective.'

'I would like to show you a short video clip from our holy Bible. It might help you to understand a bit more,' said Tom.

He walked over to a DVD player on a table on the side and pressed the 'start' button. Immediately, the story of the trial, scourging, crucifixion, death, burial and resurrection of Christ taken from this portion of Luke's Gospel was projected onto a large, white sheet pinned onto one of the walls of the tent. A careful observer would have noted that a second wire from the back of the DVD player went over the wall and downstairs into the window of the *majlis*. There, it was connected to another projector so that the men on the roof and the women in the *majlis* could watch the same movie clip at the same time.

While Tom was telling the story of the general who gave his life to save the disobedient soldier, in the *majlis* below, Hannah told the story of the woman caught in adultery from John's Gospel. Tom and Hannah often used biblical stories and parables to convey biblical truths.

The scourging, crown of thorns and crucifixion scenes were so graphic they evoked tears from some of the two audiences. A few even looked away to avoid seeing the violence. 'I didn't realise that Jesus suffered so much,' Amina later told Hannah.

But now, it was time for the food, which had just arrived hot from the restaurant. Large communal plates of aromatic rice piled high with goat meat and garnished with vegetables were placed in the centre of each group of six or so men or women. They ate enthusiastically, plunging their hands into the rice, talking animatedly with each other as they did so.

After the meal, spiced sweets, dates and fruit, and sweet tea were served. When they had eaten their fill, the guests got up to wash their hands in a sink in the corner, using washing powder to take the oil from the mutton off their hands. As they sat down, the music started again, and the singing and dancing resumed.

At about midnight, the last guests left, and Tom and Hannah cleaned up as much as they could before dropping into bed exhausted. Before they slept, they discussed what the outcomes of the evening might be. However, the events of the next week would produce results they did not expect and certainly did not want.

12. Do You Really Want To Be Free?

The morning after the rooftop party, Tom and Hannah were woken up by shouting in the street outside their house. Looking out the window, they saw a small group of men and women who were arguing vehemently with Yousef and Umar. Several times, people from the group pointed angrily towards Tom and Hannah's house.

'It looks like it's about us,' said Tom. 'I should go down there and find out.'

'No, let Yousef and Umar deal with it,' said Hannah. 'They will know better what to say and do. We are still newcomers here.'

Tom reluctantly agreed. However, that evening, he went over to their place for a scheduled evening of cards and *shisha*. Once they began playing, Tom asked them what had happened in the morning outside their house.

'A couple of disgruntled partygoers,' laughed Yousef. 'I think they were disappointed that you didn't serve any beer last night.'

Tom doubted this. *The people who were complaining had long beards or wore black burqas – not the beer-drinking types*, he thought.

'No, tell him the truth. Those idiots wouldn't know what beer tasted like!' said Umar.

'OK,' said Yousef. 'They were upset. They said that you were preaching your religion, and that you didn't have the right to do that, because this is a Muslim country. They said that you were really a missionary and had come to corrupt their children at the university.'

Tom immediately felt sick. Perhaps he had gone too far. Yousef and Umar were both looking at him intently. He wondered what to say next. He decided to go for a soft option. 'What … er … what did you say to them?' he asked.

'We told them that the Qur'an says that there is no compulsion in religion. It teaches that nearest in love to the Muslims are those who say they are Christians. We asked them why they were so insecure in their faith that they felt that Islam would collapse due to the words of one person, even if he was a missionary,' said Yousef.

'And I asked them why they were fearful for their children. I said, "If they haven't got the brains to deal with different ideas, then why did you send them to university?"' Both Yousef and Umar laughed again.

'What did they say to that?' Tom asked.

'Nothing,' said Yousef. 'They had no response because they hadn't thought about it.'

'They haven't thought about much at all,' said Umar. 'They are just like sheep, following the moron sheikhs wherever they go.'

There was a silence, then Umar spoke up, frowning. 'Tom, you have to be a bit careful. You have earned yourself some powerful enemies. Watch your back.'

Tom left at the end of the evening totally crestfallen. When he got home, Hannah was already asleep. He had to wait until the next morning to tell her about this.

'Don't worry, darling,' she said. 'God called us to this. Remember the words of Shadrach, Meshach and Abednego.'

Tom wondered what the three friends of the Old Testament prophet Daniel had to do with this. They had been taken into exile in Babylon, where they were sentenced to death for refusing to bow down to a golden idol set up by the Babylonian king.

Hannah opened up her Bible. 'This is what they said just before they were thrown into the fiery furnace, "King Nebuchadnezzar, we do not need to defend ourselves before you in this matter. If we are thrown into the blazing furnace, the God we serve is able to deliver us from it, and he will deliver us from Your Majesty's hand. But even if he does not, we want you to know, Your Majesty, that we will not serve your gods or worship the image of gold you have set up".[1] God can protect us in life and in death.'

Tom felt grateful for Hannah's faith and level-headedness in this challenging situation. But neither of them realised that her words had a prophetic touch about them.

*

---

[1] Dan 3:16–18.

Tom continued to teach at the university. He became a bit more cautious about sharing his faith, and the opportunities for such sharing seemed to dry up. He concentrated on his classes and observed good progress among his students. He began to include more English in his lectures, and he found that their English language skills were improving. The mid-year results were encouraging. Improvement was taking place.

Then, one day, the secretary came into his office. 'Doctor Tom, the dean wants to see you straight away.'

Tom walked over to the dean's office. Professor Ramzi was sitting at his large desk, which was empty apart from a single piece of paper in the middle. He looked worried. 'This fax arrived this morning,' he said, handing it to Tom.

Tom read it. 'We are the forty-first brigade of Al-Qaeda. We know that you have American agents teaching at your university. Tell them to leave within forty-eight hours, or we will send them home in body bags. And tell them to take their filthy wives with them. You have been warned.'

'But it doesn't apply to me. I'm not American,' said Tom.

'According to these guys, all Westerners are *amreeki*. In the past, they were all called *franji*, Frenchmen, a leftover from the French mandates in Lebanon and Syria,' said the dean.

'How viable a threat is this?' asked Tom.

'Hard to say,' replied the dean. 'We know that there are Al-Qaeda training camps in the south. And last week, a US drone strike killed several of their commanders. This could be in response to that.'

'So, what should we do?' asked Tom.

'We will beef up security at the university. But you need to take some precautions. Go home a different way and at different times each day. Don't answer your front door to strangers. Avoid other gatherings with foreigners. Keep a low profile. Try to avoid public places.'

'The last one will be a bit difficult,' said Tom.

'Send your servants out to do the shopping,' suggested the dean.

'We don't have servants,' said Tom.

'Then be a real Yemeni man. Put your wife into a burqa, and send her out to shop,' laughed the dean.

Tom left the office feeling unsettled. A bigger problem for him and Hannah would be avoiding gatherings with foreigners. Every Friday morning, they attended the Sana'a International Fellowship that met in a large restaurant in the centre of the city. Christians from Africa, Asia, the Middle East and some North Americans and Europeans met for worship, teaching and fellowship. It was a spiritual lifeline for them. This would be hard to give up. In the end, they decided to keep attending. The following Friday, they turned up and found that the numbers were down. It seems that many other organisations and employers and embassies had received the same fax. This made Tom feel a little bit safer, realising that it was not himself that was being targeted.

A month later, Tom received a phone call from a leader in the Sana'a International Fellowship. 'Some tragic news. Do you know Andy McLachlan? The American guy who set up a home for kids with cerebral palsy?'

'Yes, I know him well. What's happened?' asked Tom.

'We've just heard that he has been shot dead. He was on the way to the home with a load of groceries and two men on a motorcycle pulled alongside him and opened fire. He died immediately. He leaves a wife and two small children. The memorial service will be next Friday,' said the leader.

Tom told Hannah that night when she arrived home from the clinic. She immediately burst into tears. They knew Andy and Marie and their two sons very well. They had a meal with them only two weeks prior. As they were speaking, there was a knock at the front gate.

Tom went to the intercom near the front door, pressed the button and asked, 'Who is it?'

'It's me,' came the reply. Tom recognised Mahmoud's voice. He pressed the button to unlock the gate. He heard the gate open and then shut and a few seconds later there was a knock at the door. He opened it and let Mahmoud in. He took him upstairs to the *majlis*. Hannah brought them two glasses of orange juice and a bowl of fruit, and sat down with them.

'I was so sorry to hear about the American who was killed. Did you know him?' asked Mahmoud.

'Yes, he was our friend. He and his wife and children,' said Tom.

'He was doing good work. His centre was famous in our city,' said Mahmoud. 'Al-Qaeda has released a statement claiming responsibility. They said they wanted to clean the filth from our land … it is pretty obvious to me who the real filth is. They are animals.'

'Why would they choose him?' asked Hannah.

'He was a soft target, American, high profile. Lots of good, or bad, reasons,' replied Mahmoud. 'Al-Qaeda claimed he was forcing the children to convert to Christianity.'

'Well, I know that's not true,' said Tom. 'I've been to that centre several times. There is no pressure placed on those kids. Most of them are severely brain-damaged and can't talk. All of them have been abandoned by their families. Andy and his wife had picked up some of them as infants on rubbish heaps.'

'The facts don't appear to matter in cases like this. Rumour is much more attractive. But what about you? Will you leave? I have heard that some foreigners have resigned from their jobs or are sending their families home. What will you do?' asked Mahmoud.

'I'll tell you a story,' said Tom, smiling.

'How predictable!' responded Mahmoud.

'There was once a king, who ruled over a large kingdom,' began Tom, 'His rule was just and wise and his kingdom was peaceful and prosperous. All the people loved the king and were happy to live in his kingdom. However, in a neighbouring kingdom, there was another king who was vicious and evil. He was so jealous of the good king that he would do anything he could to destroy that kingdom and its king.

'One night, he sent his soldiers and kidnapped as many people as they could, forcing hundreds of them to march back to his castle. He imprisoned them in stone cells in a large dungeon beneath his castle, and began to torture them.

'The next morning, the good king heard what had happened. A messenger came from the evil king. He said that the good king must come alone and unarmed, or the evil king would begin executing ten of the prisoners every day, starting from tomorrow. If the good king came with an army, all of the prisoners would be immediately executed. The good king felt that he had no choice, so he decided to go by himself to the evil king and offer to exchange himself for the release of his people. The advisors told him that this was too dangerous and the evil king could not be trusted. But the king was more willing to risk his own safety rather than that of his imprisoned people.

'That day, the good king, alone and unarmed, set out for the castle of the evil king. When the evil king saw him coming, he rejoiced. "Now we have him," he told his troops, "and we don't need to keep our promise to release the other prisoners."

'As soon as the good king entered the castle, the soldiers of the evil king grabbed him. They beat him up, spat on him and whipped him. Then, they bound him in chains and placed him in the lowest dungeon in the castle. They didn't realise that the good king had planned this so he could rescue his people.

'The evil king placed guards on the cell door of the good king. They laughed at his stupidity because he was now locked in the prison from which no-one had ever escaped. Each day, the guards went into his cell to torture him.

'But after three days, something changed. The soldiers entered the good king's cell and found that he had broken off his chains. He overpowered the guards and took their weapons and the keys. Then, he proceeded to open the doors of every other prisoner, saying, "Follow me if you want to be free. We can fight our way out of here. It may cost some of us our lives, but freedom is better than slavery. It is better to die on our feet than to live on our knees." But many of the king's subjects decided to stay in their cells, fearing they would suffer worse torture if they were ever recaptured by the evil king.

LIBERATION IS OFFERED.
WILL THEY TAKE IT?

'However, others picked up the weapons of the guards and followed him. They said, "Our good king has absorbed all the worst that the evil king can do. He is stronger and wiser than the evil king, and we will not remain prisoners. We are going with him to find freedom."

'They followed him closely, all the way out of the prison. They imitated the way he opened the cell doors of other prisoners, and how he fought the guards. Some of the king's subjects lost their lives in the fighting. But, eventually most of them were able to make their way, following their king, back to his kingdom of righteousness and peace. Those who died on the way were honoured as martyrs. But those who remained behind in the cells were doomed to lives of imprisonment and slavery.'

Mahmoud looked at Tom. 'That is an interesting story of heroism, sacrifice and victory. But I can't see how that it is related to you and your wife staying or going.'

'Well,' said Tom. 'Like the people in the cells with the doors opened, we have a choice. Will we follow our saviour even though it may be dangerous, and strive towards freedom, or remain living in prisons of fear? If everyone who felt afraid abandoned Yemen, where would that leave the country? Hannah and I have some skills that can contribute to the development of Yemeni people. We want to stay as long as we can to help.'

'That's great,' said Mahmoud. 'And I can see that this comes from your Christian beliefs.'

'Yes,' said Hannah. 'We have a heavenly king, Jesus, who was willing to come down to earth, and to suffer and even die so that we can be free. He put his own life at risk in order to save others. If we want to follow him, we must be ready to pay the same price for the sake of others. Andy McLachlan and his wife knew the dangers of working here, but they considered the cost worth the reward that God gives those who obey him.'

'I see,' said Mahmoud.

Then Hannah stood up and said, 'I'm sorry I will have to excuse myself. I have an early start tomorrow and I need a good night's sleep. You guys can stay here and talk more if you want to. Good night.' And off she went. Mahmoud also decided it was time to leave.

As he walked home, Mahmoud was having a change of heart. This talk had given him much to think about.

13. Wedding Bells?

Hannah set off early the next morning. Her work took her to many of the small villages around Sana'a. She was accompanied by Louise, an unmarried American nurse. Both of them wore the black burqa with colourful headscarves. There had been some fighting between the different tribes in the villages around Sana'a, and tribesmen often opened fire on vehicles that were going to an opponent's village. As a result, the government required that they have a local driver and an armed guard with them in their four-wheel drive. The two men sat in the front, one with his AK47 machine gun tucked between his legs and the other driving furiously to avoid any gunfire from hostile villagers. The two women sat in the back.

In one village, called Bani Daba, Hannah and Louise were visiting a local family. Um Hilmi, the mother of the household, served them tea and dates, and then turned to the topic of Islam. 'You both look beautiful in your hijabs. Allah is pleased with that. All that you need to do now is to accept Islam by reciting the shahada. What do you think, Sister Louise? Then we could find you a nice Muslim husband.'

Louise was more than prepared for this. She had been asked many times before.

'I have a couple of problems with that,' she said. 'Firstly, why should I need to get married?'

'Our holy Prophet Muhammad taught us that *azzawwaj nifs addin*, "marriage is half of religion",' replied Um Hilmi. 'If you get married, you will have fulfilled half of Allah's requirements for you to enter Paradise.'

'Hmm … interesting. Our holy Prophet, Jesus, is already in Paradise and he never got married. So, he didn't need to. I don't want to follow a religion that considers me only half a person because I am not married. I would prefer to follow someone who regards me as a full person whether I am married or not. Secondly, I have been told that a Muslim man can marry a Christian or Jewish woman, so I wouldn't need to convert to Islam to marry your son.'

'That's true,' said Um Hilmi, smiling at the prospect. 'And my son would make a wonderful husband.'

'So, would it be OK for my brother, who is a Christian, to marry your daughter?' asked Louise.

'No, that is not allowed in Islam. He would have to convert to Islam first,' replied Um Hilmi firmly.

'Well, how is that fair? You have one rule for men and another for women. I want to follow a religion that treats everyone equally. And there is another thing. Your prophet Muhammad once said to the Muslim women, "You are defective (*naaqis*) in your intelligence and your religion."[1] As a Christian, I am equal to a man – not lacking in any way. Why would I choose to become "defective"? As a Christian, I am entitled to a full inheritance, equal to my brothers in Christ. But as a Muslim, I would receive only half under Islamic law.[2] Which is better – full inheritance or only half? I don't consider myself to be defective, or half a male. And why should my witness in court be worth only half that of a man's testimony?[3] My observation skills and honesty are at least as good any Yemeni man's. Don't you agree?'

Unhappy at this, Um Hilmi turned to Hannah.

'What about you, Doctor Hannah? Why don't you become a Muslim?'

'You just said that a Muslim woman cannot be married to a non-Muslim, so I would have to divorce my husband. But I love him and I want to stay with him, so it doesn't make sense to become a Muslim.'

Um Hilmi objected. 'But your husband might decide to become a Muslim too!'

Hannah was ready. 'Tell me, Um Hilmi. If you became a Christian, do you think your husband, Abu Hilmi, would also become a Christian? Does a man always, or ever, change his religion just because his wife did?'

'Of course not. Men make their own decisions. And Abu Hilmi would never become an unbeliever!'

Hannah continued, 'If both my husband and I became Muslims, he could marry another wife, or even two or three more. As a Christian, my husband will not marry another woman. We will remain together as a

---

1 Sahih *al-Bukahri* 1951, https://sunnah.com/bukhari:1951
2 Q 4.11.
3 Q 2.282.

couple – just the two of us. Why should I choose to share my house and my husband with other women?'

'But he can only marry another woman with your permission,' said Um Hilmi.

'Is that true? Does the Qur'an say that? Did Muhammad ever ask permission of his other wives before he married another one? No, he didn't. In fact, they were very unhappy when he took on more wives, and tried to prevent it.'

'I will have to ask my imam about that,' said Um Hilmi.

'And then, there is the question of Paradise,' Hannah continued. 'How many virgins does a man get in Paradise? Seventy-two, according to the Hadith![4] Do you think any woman would look forward to her husband having seventy-two lovers? And will the woman get seventy-two virgin men for herself? I don't think so.' Hannah found herself becoming a bit angry at the injustice of it all.

'No, you are thinking about it all in the wrong way,' said Um Hilmi.

'So, what is the right way to be thinking about it? I will tell you. We believe that God created Adam and he gave to him one wife to be with for all of their lives. Men invented polygamy for their own pleasure, contrary to God's plan. For us as Christians, marriage is a symbol of God's love for us. Christian husbands are told to love their wives in the same way that Jesus Christ loves his people. He gave his life for them,' said Hannah.

As she was speaking, she realised that Um Hilmi was tuning out. *Too many abstract concepts*, she thought. *Time for a story.*

Then, she announced confidently, 'I would not become a Muslim for the same reason that Abdul would not marry Fatima.'

'Who is Abdul? Who is Fatima? Do I know them?' asked Um Hilmi.

'Abdul was a man who lived in a village, much like this one,' said Hannah. 'He married Aisha, a woman from the city. She had been to university and became a doctor. She was a beautiful woman and Abdul loved her very much. Aisha loved him very much and did everything for him. She cooked his meals and kept the house very clean and entertained his friends. As a doctor, she worked hard in a nearby clinic, so she brought home a good income as well.

---

4 *Hadith Tirmidhi*, https://sunnah.com/tirmidhi:1663

'But one day, the man's neighbour came to Abdul with a proposal. He said, "You know my daughter, Fatima."

"Yes, I know her," said Abdul. He had met her many times and he knew that she was not attractive, nor intelligent.

'Fatima's father went on, "Fatima is causing lots of trouble at home. She doesn't like housework or cooking, so she doesn't do any. She didn't finish school and she doesn't want to get a job. And she doesn't like visitors coming around. She is always fighting with my wife, so our household is like a war zone."

"So, why are telling me this? What does this have to do with me?" asked Abdul.

'Fatima's father explained, "Now, she wants to get married. She has seen how you treat your wife and she is very impressed. So, she said she wants to marry you. But she could not cope with any competition in the house. She said that first you must first divorce your wife, Aisha, and then she would accept you. What do you say? Would you like to marry my daughter?"'

ABDUL IS GIVEN AN OFFER TOO BAD TO ACCEPT.

Hannah turned to Um Hilmi, whose mouth was agape at this story. Hannah asked, 'If you were Abdul, what would you say?'

'What an atrocious offer,' she exploded. 'How could Fatima's father even think that his proposal would be accepted? It is a ridiculous idea. Abdul would be silly to divorce Aisha and marry Fatima.'

Hannah smiled. 'Yes, I agree with you. If you have something good, you should not give it up for something that is not as good. As a Christian, I follow Jesus Christ. He loves me – in fact, so much that he gave his life for me. I can speak to him at any time in my own language. We have a rich relationship together. It is like we are married in a spiritual way. He provides everything that I could ever wish for. He is the perfect partner.'

Then she paused, frowned and went on, 'But now you want me to leave Christ and abandon his love for me. You want me to follow Muhammad. You want me to pray five times a day in a foreign language that I struggle to speak. You want me to read the Qur'an in an ancient Arabic language I don't understand. You expect me to go to Mecca with two million people I don't know, and be required to go without food and drink every day for one month every year until I die. Why would I ever want to do all that?'

Um Hilmi was taken aback by the force of this argument. She was also impressed by the strength with which Hannah spoke it. In Arab culture, presenting a strong argument in a powerful way is a sign of conviction and truth. It was something to be admired; Hannah clearly thought that what she said was true. Um Hilmi had no way of refuting this. She quickly changed the topic and began talking about some other events that had been taking place in the village.

But she had some serious questions that she was going to ask Abu Hilmi when he got home from the fields that night.

As Hannah and Louise settled down for the night in Um Hilmi's *majlis*, they could hear the vigorous discussion between Abu Hilmi and Um Hilmi in the next room. Before she drifted off to sleep, Hannah wondered what Tom was doing that night.

14. Doing the Right Thing

Hannah would sometimes be away for several nights at a time during her village visits with Louise, while Tom remained in Sana'a. During the days, he was teaching at the university. However, he missed Hannah's company. Mobile phone coverage did not extend to the small villages in the mountains, so all he could do was pray that Hannah and Louise were safe.

So, each evening, he would go to Yousef and Umar's house next door to talk, play cards and smoke *shisha*. The friendship was becoming deeper, and Yousef and Umar often asked insightful questions. They had clearly been thinking about the rooftop party, and the other things they had heard from Tom.

Yousef began, 'Doctor Tom, we enjoy the stories that you tell us.'

'What do you understand from them?' asked Tom, keen to know what take-home messages they had gleaned.

'The first day we met, you told us the story of the son and the slave, and how the slave had to work to stay in the palace, but the son was guaranteed a place there, because of his relationship to the king,' said Yousef.

'Then at the rooftop party, you told the story of the general who saved your life even though you had disobeyed his orders,' said Umar.

'That's right,' responded Tom. 'And what did you conclude from those stories?'

'We like the concept of grace. As you know, we are not very good Muslims. On the day of judgement, if there is such a day, we will both fare badly. Your concept of someone powerful, whether a king, accepting us because of who we are, or a general, acting to save us when we have been foolish, is very attractive,' said Yousef.

'Yes, and we also like the lack of rules,' said Umar. 'Islam is full of rules. They are so hard to keep. Most Muslims do not keep them – we have given up even trying. The best rules are no rules!'

'Christianity is very attractive to us. We like the idea that we can keep getting drunk every night, and Umar can keep his Elsa,' said Yousef, pointing to the large poster of the topless woman behind the door, 'and no-one will judge us.'

Tom immediately felt overcome with embarrassment. He had clearly left these two men with the wrong impression. 'No, no. I think you might have misunderstood me,' Tom said. 'There is a difference between being saved by grace and being saved by works. Being saved does not mean that good works are completely absent. It is a matter of chronology.'

'What do you mean?' asked Umar.

'Imagine a man was travelling an ocean cruise. One day, he was standing too close to a rail, leaning over, and he fell overboard,' said Tom.

'Probably drunk. We both got drunk every day when we went on a cruise,' said Yousef.

'Possibly,' said Tom. 'But he survived the fall into the water, only to see the cruise ship disappearing off into the distance. He had booked into the cruise by himself, and didn't know anyone else on board, so he guessed that no-one would miss him for a long time. He looked around and could see nothing but water. He was in the middle of a vast ocean. No land was in sight. Even if he was a good long-distance swimmer, which he was not, he wouldn't know which direction to go. He stayed in one place, treading water.

'As the day went on, he became more and more tired. He was also hungry and thirsty and cold. He wondered how much longer he could survive. Then suddenly, he heard a noise. He turned around and saw a fishing boat in the distance going past. He yelled and waved his arms, using his last reserves of energy. And then he saw the boat begin to turn around. It approached him slowly and a fisherman reached out and pulled him aboard.

'They gave him dry clothes, and food and drink. The saved man said, "I am so glad you found me. Another couple of hours and I would have drowned. What can I do to repay you?"

'The captain replied, "Well, we are a fishing vessel. We will be fishing for several days before we return to port. Would you like to help us? I will pay you the same wages as the rest of the crew. It will be hard work, but we could use the help."

Then Tom stopped and said, "What do you think the man will say?"

Umar replied for both of them, 'Of course he will help them. They saved his life. He would even work for nothing. He owes them big-time.'

'But, what if he refused? What if he said, "No, I don't want to help you. I will just sit in the boat and eat your food and drink your tea?" What should the captain do?' asked Tom.

'I think he should throw the lazy so-and-so overboard,' said Yousef.

'Can you see the parallel?' asked Tom. 'If you put your trust in Christ and he saves you by his death on the cross, you owe him a massive debt of gratitude. And then, he calls us to follow him and to become involved in his task of taking this good news to the world, in caring for others as he did, and living holy lives.'

'Well, that would really make a difference in the world,' said Umar. 'If everyone took this seriously, it would be revolutionary.'

'I'm not pretending it would be easy,' said Tom. 'Jesus said that the way is hard and the road that leads to life is narrow, and those who find it are few.[1] There are tough decisions that would need to be made by anyone who decides to follow Jesus.'

'Do you mean we could have to give up alcohol?' asked Yousef. 'Is your God opposed to alcohol?'

'Well, Jesus turned water into wine,[2] said Tom. 'So, alcohol is not completely forbidden, as it is in Islam. But we are told in the Holy Bible not to become drunk with wine,[3] so a boundary has been set. And it also says that "all things are lawful, but not all things are beneficial".[4] If alcohol is affecting you negatively in any way – financially, physically, socially – you need to have a good think about how much of it you drink.'

'What about Elsa?' asked Umar, pointing to the large poster. 'Would I have to get rid of her?'

'Jesus had some important things to say about lust,' said Tom. 'He said, "If your eye causes you to sin, pluck it out,"[5] and "whoever has looked at a woman lustfully has already committed adultery with her in his heart".[6] Jesus set some lofty standards for our behaviour.'

'Wow, those are very high bars,' said Yousef. 'I'm not sure if I could jump that high.'

'But God does not leave you to do this all by yourself,' said Tom. 'He sends his Holy Spirit into your life to help you and guide you. You are not abandoned to struggle on alone. There is also the support of other Christians, who are called the Body of Christ.'

'All the same, there are many things to consider,' said Umar. 'The legal implications fare immensely – apostasy merits a death sentence in this country. If the government won't carry it out, Al-Qaeda would. You saw what they did to the American orphanage guy. They wouldn't think twice

---

1 Matt 7:14.
2 John 2:1–11.
3 Eph 5:18.
4 1 Cor 6:12; 10:23.
5 Matt 5:29.
6 Matt 5:28.

about doing that, or worse, to us. We'd lose our jobs at the very least, and our families would disown us. How would we live?'

He pondered for a moment, and then dropped his head. 'I'm sorry, Doctor Tom, the price is too high.'

YOUSEF AND UMAR COUNT THE COST.

Tom didn't know what to say. He knew they were right. Any public conversion would attract a lot of negative attention and certain opposition. The price was huge. He thought of Jesus' parable about the man who found a treasure buried in a plot of land. The man sold everything in order to buy that land. But for some people, the risks of making such a purchase seemed too great.

Tom took his leave from Yousef and Umar. He walked home sadly. When he arrived at his house, he saw a figure standing in the darkness. The figure spoke up, 'Doctor Tom, could I have a word with you?' The figure stepped out of the darkness into the light of a street lamp.

It was Abdul Kareem whose son had been throwing rocks at Tom's house. He continued, 'I have some important questions about the meeting on your rooftop. Could you and your wife come to my house for dinner tomorrow night?'

Tom's spirits rose. This sounded like some genuine interest. 'Of course we will come. What time?'

'Please come at sunset,' said Abdul Kareem. And he walked off.

15. The Lifesaver Who Could Not Swim

The next morning, Hannah came home full of enthusiasm about her trip with Louise to Bani Daba. She excitedly told Tom about all that had happened. He talked about his evening with Yousef and Umar, and the invitation from Abdul Kareem. They prayed together, thanking God for what had taken place and asking for wisdom for that evening.

At sunset, they walked, again hand-in-hand, to Abdul Kareem and Amina's house. Abdul Kareem greeted them warmly. He took Tom by the hand and led him into the long *majlis*. Tom had expected this to be a private, one-on-one affair. Instead, about twenty men were seated in the room, reclining against the walls on the mattress-type cushions. The only spare seat was beside the bearded imam at the far end of the long room. Tom had often listened to his fiery sermons broadcast through the public loudspeakers into their neighbourhood. The imam motioned Tom to sit down beside him.

Meanwhile, Hannah had been taken to another room where six women were seated in a circle on the floor. Hannah was shown a cushion in the circle, and she sat on it. Amina opened up the proceedings. 'What do you think of our Islam?' she asked Hannah.

Hannah was a bit taken aback by the abruptness of this question. She wondered how to respond appropriately. She decided on a diplomatic approach. 'All religions are attempts by people to draw close to God,' Hannah answered. 'Many religions have teachings which provide comfort to their followers.'

'Yes, but Islam is the final religion, because Muhammad is the final prophet. No other prophet will come after him,' declared another lady. She was heavy-set with thick, black eyebrows. Hannah had seen her visiting the houses in the area, always accompanied by a group of other women. She thought that she might be a Qur'an teacher.

'Let me tell you a story,' said Hannah, 'and then I will ask you a question.'

'OK,' said the woman. She looked very confident.

'There was a man who had three sons: an older son, a middle son and a younger son,' said Hannah. 'Unfortunately, there was a car accident and the older son and the younger son were killed. Which son would be the last son?'

'The one that was still alive, of course,' said the woman.

'Correct. And as you know, all of the prophets, from Adam to Muhammad, have died and we know where the tombs of many of them are. David's tomb is in Jerusalem, Job's tomb is in Salalah in Oman, Muhammad's tomb is in Medina. But where is Jesus' tomb?' asked Hannah.

'Jesus doesn't have a tomb,' replied the woman. 'Jesus is not dead. He is alive.'

'So, if all the other prophets are dead, and Jesus is still alive, then, according to your earlier statement, Jesus must be the last prophet,' replied Hannah. 'So, I follow him because he is the last prophet.'

The woman smiled in an embarrassed way. She had no response to this.

Hannah continued, 'And who is coming back on the last day? Will it be Moses, or Muhammad, or Jesus?'

'Jesus,' stated the woman.

'So, if Jesus is coming back on the last day, and he is still alive now, then he must be the last prophet. That's why I follow Jesus. No-one can come after him,' announced Hannah triumphantly.

The women looked dumbfounded. They had not expected this.

In the men's *majlis*, Tom was receiving a similar grilling. The imam gave a short sermon on the benefits of Islam and the possibility of Paradise for those who submitted to Allah. He concluded with, 'So I would like to invite you to embrace Islam.'

Tom leaned backwards. He realised that he was outnumbered twenty to one, they were all armed and he was not, and it was a long way to the front door. He also took a diplomatic approach. He said, 'Thank you, Imam, for your kind invitation. I am sure that you believe all the things that you have just told me. However, I am already a follower of Jesus Christ. He gave his life for me and he has saved me, and I am content with him.'

'But what about Muhammad?' the imam asked. 'We accept Jesus as a prophet, why don't you accept Muhammad as a prophet?'

Everyone leaned forward. They wanted to know what this foreigner thought. 'The answer is simple,' Tom said. 'Let me tell you a story. There was a man who was driving to a village that he hadn't visited before. He came to a fork in the road. He was unsure which way to go – left or right. Fortunately, there were two people at the crossroads. One of them had been before to the village he was going to, and that person was alive. The second person had never been to that village, and he was lying dead on the side of the road. Who do you think the traveller should ask; the live person, or the dead one?'

'The live person who had been there before, obviously. There would be no use asking the dead man,' said the imam.

'What you say is true,' said Tom. 'However, both Muslims and Christians agree that Jesus is alive, and Muhammad is dead. Because of this, Muhammad cannot harm us, nor can he help us. But we agree that Jesus is coming back from heaven. So that is why I follow Jesus.'

AN OBVIOUS CHOICE.

The imam continued. 'Even though Muhammad is dead, he was still a prophet, a messenger from God.'

Tom nodded. 'Yes, you believe that, but I don't. Otherwise, I would be a Muslim. But what did Muhammad claim for himself? In the Qur'an, he says to his followers, "I am no innovation among the prophets, and I do not know what will happen to me or what will happen to you".[1] Muhammad, as great a man as he was, did not know whether he would enter Paradise or not. Whereas Jesus says, "I am the way, the truth, and the life. No-one comes to the Father except by me".[2] Muhammad claimed to bring nothing new, and Jesus came to show the way to heaven.'

The widespread frowns showed Tom that this idea was not accepted. The imam spoke for them all, 'No, everyone must get to heaven by their works. No-one can be the mediator for anyone else.'[3]

'That's interesting,' Tom replied, 'because I have been reading the Hadith, the sayings of the prophet recorded by his companions. One day, Muhammad said, "The good deeds of any person will not make him enter Paradise." (In other words, none can enter Paradise through his good deeds.)

'The Prophet's companions said, "Not even you, O Allah's Apostle?"

'He said, "Not even myself, unless Allah bestows His favour and mercy (*rahma*) on me".[4]

This saying was well-known because several of the listeners recited the last sentence along with Tom. He continued, 'And who, according to the Qur'an, is the mercy (*rahma*) of God?'

'Muhammad?' suggested Abdul Kareem.

'No, it can't be Muhammad, because he will be searching for the "mercy of God". This is one of the titles of Jesus.[5] Just like Muhammad, each one of us needs Jesus, the mercy of God, in order to be saved. On the day of judgement, you and me and everyone else, including Muhammad, will be looking for Jesus, the mercy of God. The question is, will it be too late then?

---

1 Q 46.9.

2 John 14:6.

3 Q 74.48.

4 *Sahih al-Bukhari* 5673, https://sunnah.com/bukhari:5673

5 Q 19.13.

It is clear that there is no other way but Jesus. God is one, and the path of salvation is one.'

The room went silent.

In the women's room, the noise was overwhelming. The discussion about Muhammad being the last prophet was becoming heated.

'Well,' said the heavy-set woman. 'Even if Jesus is coming back, he is not on earth now. Muhammad was the last prophet on earth historically. He came last of all.'

Hannah had a response to this. 'Coming last is not always the best thing. Let me tell you a story. A woman was swimming in the sea. But the waves became big and the strong tide began to pull her out away from the shore. Soon she found that she was having difficulty. She struggled and panicked and began to drown.

'Fortunately, at that moment, another woman on the beach saw her. This woman was a powerful swimmer. She dived into the water and swam out to the drowning woman. She said, "Don't panic. Just relax. I will save you."

'The powerful swimmer held the drowning woman's head out of the water with one hand, and paddled back to shore with the other, moving slowly through the waves and against the tide. Eventually, they arrived at the beach, exhausted, but both alive. They were panting hard.

'Just then, a man ran up to them. He was wearing a T-shirt that said "Lifesaver". He said to the women, "I'm the official lifesaver. I have come to save you."

'The woman who had been drowning said, "You can't save me. You're too late. I've already been saved."'

COMING LAST IS NOT ALWAYS GOOD.

Some of the women giggled at this.

'Then the woman asked the man, "Your T-shirt looks very new, like it's never been in the water. Can you even swim?" The lifesaver looked embarrassed. "I don't know. I've never tried."

At this, the women giggled even more. One said, 'A lifesaver who couldn't swim? That's ridiculous.'

Hannah went on, 'Then the woman asked him, "So how do think you could save me, when you are not even sure you could save yourself?"'

The room went quiet.

Hannah continued, 'Sometimes, coming last means coming too late. Just because a religion comes last does not mean that it meets our needs. And, if you are in a race, you do not want to come last! And if you want to save others, you have to be strong enough to save yourself first.'

She turned to the heavy-set woman, 'You said that Muhammad came last historically, but he also brought nothing new.[6] Jesus has already saved

---

6 Q 46.9.

us. He gives us forgiveness, peace and eternal life. Muhammad could not guarantee any of those for us because he could not even guarantee them for himself. He said to his own tribe, his own family, his own daughter, "Save yourselves. I cannot save you."[7]

'But Muhammad was a great man. There has never been anyone else like him,' said Amina.

'I'm not so sure that he was that unique,' said Hannah. 'Let me tell you what I know about Muhammad. He was born just like you and I, with a father named Abdullah and mother named Amina. He said he was just a normal man.[8] He was uneducated and illiterate.[9] He lived like you and me – he got married and had children. He admitted that he did not know the future,[10] and, according to the Qur'an, he never performed any miracles.[11] He asked for forgiveness for his sins seventy[12] or one hundred[13] times a day. He didn't obey God's laws perfectly, just like you and I don't. He died for his own sins, just like you and I will. He is buried in a grave in Medina, just as you and I will be buried in a grave. His body is awaiting the day of resurrection, just like you and I will be one day. He will stand before God on the Day of Judgment, just like you and I.'

'Yes, we believe all of these things,' said Amina.

'But it is significant that Jesus is different in every one of these respects. He was born miraculously without a human father. He was educated and literate. He did not get married or have children, but he did know the future. According to the Qur'an and the Bible, Jesus performed many miracles of different kinds. He never had to ask forgiveness for his sins because he did not have any. He lived a pure and perfect life. When he died, he died not for his own sins, but for the sins of the world. He was buried in a tomb, but three days later, he rose from the dead. His grave is empty. His glorified body is now in heaven, seated at the right hand of God the Father. Jesus will

---

7 *Sahih al-Bukhari* 2753, https://sunnah.com/bukhari:2753

8 Q 7.61.

9 Q 7.158.

10 Q 6.50; 11.33; 46.9.

11 Q 6.109; 17.92–98; 21.3, 5, 10; 29.49.

12 *Sahih al-Bukhari* 6307, https://sunnah.com/bukhari:6307

13 *Sahih Muslim* 2707, https://sunnah.com/muslim:2702a

not face judgement – he will be the judge. Every person will be judged on how they have responded to Jesus.'

The room went silent again. The heavy-set woman had had enough. She stood up. 'Well, it is clear that you either do not understand our religion or you choose not to accept it. But we have conveyed to you what we believe. I can see no further value in talking with you. I must go now. Good evening.'

She went around the women, kissing them on both cheeks. When she got to Hannah, instead of kissing her, she looked at her and said, 'May Allah guide you to the truth.'

'Thank you,' replied Hannah. 'Praise God, he already has.'

The woman walked out. One by one, the others got up and followed her, leaving Hannah and Amina alone in an uncomfortable silence.

Hearing the sounds of the door opening, and footsteps departing, Tom concluded that the women's meeting was over. He decided it was time for them to leave. He stood up and went around the room, shaking hands with the men and kissing each one on both cheeks, as is the local custom. He asked their forgiveness if he had offended anyone, which they all assured him was not the case.

As Tom was leaving, one of the men came and asked if he could give him a DVD of the gospel, just like he had given one to Abdul Kareem at the end of the rooftop meeting. Tom asked him to come around to his house the next day to collect it.

The following morning, the man came. Tom invited him inside to have a drink, but he refused. Instead, he simply asked for a copy of the *Jesus* DVD. When Tom brought it, the man quickly put it into his bag and hurried away. Tom thought the man might have been concerned about the neighbours seeing him carrying Christian materials, so he was trying to minimise his exposure. As Tom would learn later, the man's reasons were much more sinister.

16. Betrayed

After that evening meeting, things began to change. The first sign was the weekly sermon from the mosque, broadcast by loudspeaker into the whole neighbourhood. It started the next Friday. The *imam* became even fiercer in his preaching. He spoke against those who 'come to our country to mislead our people and pervert our religion and ruin our morals.' Tom never heard his own name mentioned, but as the only Westerners living in the area, it seemed obvious whom the *imam* was referring to. Tom and Hannah noticed that the local people seemed a bit less friendly and willing to engage. People walked past them on the street without greeting them or even looking at them. Previously Hannah had received invitations from the local women to drink tea, cook, or go shopping together. These stopped.

At the university, some of the staff began to avoid Tom. His classes were getting smaller, and the once-enthusiastic students were less willing to hang around and talk with Tom after class.

One day, Tom received an unexpected phone call.

'Hi Tom, it's Eamon. Remember me? We studied Arabic together in the Old City.'

'Yes, Eamon – of course I remember you. How are things going?'

'Very well. Our NGO is growing. Lots of things happening. How about for you?'

'OK, I suppose. I'm still teaching at the university. Hannah is involved in a medical outreach project in some villages and has a small clinic at home,' replied Tom.

'Yes, I heard about that. Very important work. I hope she can keep it up … Hey, Tom, I have heard some other things. Our local NGO staff spend a lot of time in government offices getting papers signed and such things. They have reported some disturbing news about you.'

Tom gulped hard. 'Wh-what kind of news?' he asked.

'It's nothing specific, and that's what's disturbing. The government officials keep asking our employees if we have anything to do with you, and if we know anything about you. We plead ignorance, of course. But there is one other thing,' said Eamon.

'What's that?' asked Tom.

'Yesterday, one of my employees saw a file with your name on it in the Ministry of the Interior. He said it was over an inch thick – apparently they have collected a lot of information about you.'

'Is that a problem?' asked Tom. 'They collect information about everyone.'

'Yes, they do,' said Eamon. 'But the story is that as soon as a file gets over an inch thick, they can't be bothered reading through it all, so they kick the person out.'

'Is that true?' asked Tom.

'It's just a story, but there might be some truth to it. Anyway, I thought I would give you a heads-up on this.'

'Thanks for that. I appreciate it,' said Tom.

'No problems. Please give my regards to Hannah. Goodbye.' Eamon hung up.

Tom felt sick. He didn't know what to do. Perhaps it was all rumours and fearmongering. But he was concerned about the other changes he was observing. He told Hannah about the phone call when she came home that night. She went white. 'Let's pray,' she said.

They prayed together, asking God for wisdom and to calm their nerves. When they finished Hannah said, 'At least we know that God is in control. No matter what happens, he is working out his purposes.'

They went to bed, but neither of them slept well that night.

The next morning, there was a loud knock at the front gate. Tom went to the intercom. 'Who is it?' he asked.

'The police!' came back a gruff voice. 'Open the gate!'

Tom went to the front gate, slid back the bolt and opened it. There stood two policemen in uniform. 'Are you Doctor Tom?' one of them asked.

'Yes, I am,' said Tom.

'We would like you to come down to the police station with us,' said the policeman.

'Why?' asked Tom. 'Has something happened?'

'We have only been told to bring you to the police station,' the policeman replied.

'Wait a minute. I have to tell my wife, then I will come back,' said Tom. He closed the gate, and slid the bolt shut and walked inside.

Hannah had been listening from the front door. 'Are they arresting you?' she asked.

'I don't think so. It might just be about our visas. They are about to expire. Probably an administrative matter,' said Tom, hopefully. But inside, he doubted it.

Hannah was prepared. She went to the bathroom, got Tom's toothbrush and a tube of toothpaste. She picked up a small New Testament from the bedroom and came back to Tom, stuffing them in his pocket. 'In case they put you in prison,' she explained. 'Now, give me your wallet so they can't take your money or your credit card.' Tom handed over his wallet. He was feeling numb, and yet amazed at Hannah's level-headedness.

HANNAH PREPARES TOM FOR PRISON.

The police started hammering on the door again. 'Open the door!' they demanded.

Hannah kissed Tom and hugged him and said, 'I'll be praying for you.'

Tom walked out to the gate, opened it and climbed into the police car. Many of the neighbours were watching as he was driven off.

At the police station, he was taken to the captain's office. 'Doctor Tom, we have received certain reports about your activities.' He held up a thick file.

As he did so, a *Jesus* DVD fell out of the file, onto the desk. Tom immediately recognised it. He tried not to show any reaction. He asked, 'What kinds of reports? Who wrote them? What do they say?'

'I'm afraid I can't tell you. But I have been told to inform you that you and your wife must leave Yemen within three days.'

'Three days! That's impossible. We have a house full of our things. How can we even pack up in three days?'

'I'm sorry. I don't make the orders. I only carry them out. Your visa has been cancelled. My men will deal with the administration, and then take you home,' said the captain. He called a constable.

The 'administration' involved being fingerprinted on a form that said, 'expelled'. 'Does this mean I won't be able to come back to Yemen?' Tom asked the constable.

The policemen looked around to see if anyone was listening. 'Not for a very long time,' he said in a low voice.

17. An Unexpected Homecoming

When Tom returned home, he told Hannah what the police had said. She burst into tears. They hugged each other and cried together. As he thought about it, Tom became angry. 'They can't do this. We haven't committed any crimes. You can't just expel people because you don't agree with their ideas. I am going to fight this.'

'Well, you do what you think is right. But I might start packing, just in case,' said Hannah softly.

Tom arranged a meeting with the dean of the university that afternoon.

'Yes, we have received notification of the cancellation of your visa,' said the dean. 'I am so sorry. You have been a great teacher, and I will write you a good reference. But we are subject to government regulations. We have to do what they say.'

'But this is so unjust,' said Tom. 'Aren't you able to appeal?'

'This has come from high up in government,' said the dean. 'It sounds like you have made some powerful enemies. We have to think about the long-term needs of the university. We don't dare fight it. I'm so sorry.'

They shook hands and Tom left. Tom went home to find that Hannah had progressed with the packing. 'I've even booked one-way tickets to Australia for the day after next, but I haven't paid for them yet,' she said.

Tom's next port of call was the Australian embassy. Later that day, the secretary of the embassy rang him back. 'We contacted the Ministry of the Interior and they are refusing to budge on this. Clearly, you have upset someone. Ultimately, every country has the right to decide who stays and who goes. The good news is that they don't think you are a spy – spies only get two days to leave. We think it would be better for you to leave quietly, otherwise they will use force against you and you could both spend some time in prison.'

That night, there was a knock at the back gate. Tom opened it to find Yousef and Umar. 'Can we come in?' they asked, looking around nervously.

'Of course,' said Tom, ushering them inside.

'We are so sorry to hear what has happened to you,' said Umar, as they sat in the *majlis* drinking tea. 'It is unfair that people like you and your wife who come here to help our nation are told to leave, while others who come to take as much as they can are allowed to stay.'

'Thank you for your vote of confidence,' said Tom. 'We only wish that others felt the same way.'

'We also have something for you, but we are not sure what it is,' said Yousef. 'It was pushed under our front door sometime today.' He handed over a small envelope that was addressed, 'To Doctor Tom. Open in private.'

After Yousef and Umar left, Tom and Hannah opened the letter. It read, *I will see you at the airport. I have some important news.* The letter was unsigned.

'Who do you think this is from?' asked Hannah.

'I have no idea. I don't recognise the writing,' said Tom.

'Be careful,' cautioned Hannah. 'It might be a trap.'

They spent the next day packing up their stuff. Books, clothes and souvenirs were packed into cardboard boxes to be airfreighted after they left. By sunset, they were finished. After a late dinner, they went to bed, knowing that this would be their last night in Yemen. It was a very sad time.

The next morning, they got up early and had a quick breakfast. Stale flatbread and peanut butter were all they had left in the house. They took the taxi ride to the airport in silence. They wondered who would meet them there.

After they had booked in for their flights, Tom and Hannah sat in a small cafe in the departure area. It was very busy, with many people coming and going. Eventually, a man with his head wrapped in a scarf came up to them.

'Can I sit down?' he asked.

It was winter, so men with scarves swathed over their faces was not unusual. They nodded. After he sat down, he partially unwrapped the scarf so they could see his face. It was Mahmoud. He quickly re-covered his face and spoke to them in a low voice. 'I'm sorry I couldn't come to your house to say goodbye. There were unmarked police cars parked all around it. I have friends in the police and they warned me. The police followed you here this morning, but now they have gone.'

'Thank you for taking the risk,' said Tom. 'We appreciate it.'

'No, thank *you*,' said Mahmoud. 'I have learnt so much from you. I am so glad that you came to Yemen.'

'You said in the letter that you had some important news,' said Hannah curiously. 'Can you tell us what it is?'

'Yes,' said Mahmoud. 'After listening to your stories and your explanations, I have become convinced that Christianity is true, and that Islam is false. In all honesty, I can no longer follow Muhammad and Islam. I have decided to follow Jesus.'

'That's wonderful news,' said Tom. 'But be warned. It will be hard and dangerous for you.'

'Yes, I know that,' said Mahmoud. 'I am willing to pay the price if necessary. However, I will be careful. I would like to live as long as possible!'

Just then, the final call for their flight was announced over the loudspeakers. 'I have a special request for you,' said Mahmoud, 'but it can wait until you get back to Australia.'

'OK,' said Tom, 'but let me pray for you now.' And the three of them prayed together before Tom and Hannah boarded their flight. As the plane lifted off the tarmac, Tom and Hannah felt a sense of joy at Mahmoud's new faith. But they wondered what his 'special request' might be.

On arrival in Sydney, they were met by Tom's parents. They went home with them and stayed in the house where Tom grew up while they considered their future.

About a week later, Tom's phone rang. It was a Yemeni number that he did not recognise. He answered. It was Mahmoud. 'Doctor Tom, how are you? How are your parents? How is your family? How is Australia?'

'We are all very well, Mahmoud,' said Tom. 'It is wonderful to hear from you. Let me put it on speakerphone, so Hannah can hear.'

'Good,' said Mahmoud. 'Now, I will tell you both my special request.'

'What is it?' asked Hannah.

'I want to get baptised,' said Mahmoud. 'There is a lot of danger here. I am being tracked by the police all the time. I might be arrested and tortured or even killed. I want to die as a baptised Christian.'

'Is this phone call safe?' asked Tom.

'Yes it is. Remember I am studying Information Technology. We IT people know how to encrypt phone calls so no-one can listen in.'

'That's great that you want to be baptised,' said Tom. 'I can organise someone from the Sana'a International Fellowship to do it.'

'No,' said Mahmoud. 'That would be too risky, for me and for them. My house is being watched, as yours was. The police are secretly photographing everyone who comes and goes. And besides, I want you to baptise me, Doctor Tom. You are my spiritual father.'

'That's a nice idea,' said Hannah, 'but it's not practical. Tom is here, and he can't go back. And you are there. How could he baptise you?'

'Over the phone,' said Mahmoud. 'All we need is water and the Holy Spirit. I have a bottle of water. And you told me that the Holy Spirit is everywhere. So, you can baptise me over the phone. It will be a virtual baptism.' He chuckled.

'No,' said Tom. 'It's never been done before. It's not right.'

'Just because something hasn't been done before doesn't mean that it's not right,' said Mahmoud. 'Nobody had changed water into wine or walked on water before Jesus did, but it was still right!'

Hannah laughed. 'He has a point there, Tom.'

'I'm not sure,' said Tom. 'I don't want to be known as the one who invented online baptism.'

'Doctor Tom, listen to me. Is Jesus there with you? And is he here with me at the same time? Jesus said, "Wherever two or three are gathered together in my name, I am in the midst of them".[1] Today, he is using the telephone signals to bring us into one place. Let's do it. I might not be here tomorrow.'

Tom realised that all this was true, so he relented. 'OK, I give in. Let's do it. Hannah, would you pray for Mahmoud?'

'I'd love to. Let's pray. Father, we thank you that you are a God of miracles. We thank you for the miracle of new life that you have given to Mahmoud. And we thank you for mobile phones. I pray that you would bless and encourage Mahmoud as he takes this amazing step of faith. We are grateful for Mahmoud's courage and his trust in you, and for the way in which you have led him. Give him strength to follow you no matter what the cost. We pray in Jesus' name.'

---

[1] Matt 18:20.

'Amen,' said Tom. 'Now Mahmoud, start pouring the bottle of water over your head. I baptise you in the name of the Father, and of the Son and of the Holy Spirit.'

AN INTERNATIONAL ONLINE BAPTISM.

At the other end of the line, they heard Mahmoud exclaim, 'Woo hoo!' He felt that he had been washed clean and born anew.

Tom and Hannah hugged each other and Mahmoud hugged his phone. Tom then gave Mahmoud some practical ideas about how to sustain and grow his faith in Christ. They committed to stay in touch through weekly phone calls.

As they ended the call, Tom and Hannah realised that leaving Yemen was the end of a chapter of their lives. God had taken them through many different experiences and taught them many things. And there was still much for them to do in the future. Their story would continue.

However, for Mahmoud, a new story was just beginning. He had been brought home to Jesus, but this was simply the first chapter.